A LESSON FROM A MASTER

As the waltz grew ever swifter, Felicity had the strange sense that she and Justin stood still while the ballroom whirled around them. Her heart beat ever faster, until the echo of it drowned out the tinkling of the music box. She clutched Justin's shoulder more tightly, and her fingers clenched around his. His hand moved more firmly about her waist, bringing her to his broad, powerful chest.

Suddenly Justin stopped, and she swayed dizzily, not trusting her knees to hold her upright. But his strong arms supported her, and she knew no fear of falling.

Slowly, his face moved toward hers, and without thinking, she tilted back her head . . . as this lesson in the dance turned into a lesson that was far more dangerous . . .

LEIGH HASKELL explored castles, museums, and cold cities while based in Germany. She now lives with her husband and two sons in northeast Ohio and studies historically preserved homes.

SIGNET REGENCY ROMANCE
COMING IN DECEMBER 1990

Sandra Heath
A Christmas Courtship

Emma Lange
The Reforming of Lord Roth

Emily Hendrickson
Double Deceit

THE
VENGEFUL
VISCOUNT

by Leigh Haskell

A SIGNET BOOK

SIGNET
Published by the Penguin Group
Penguin Books USA Inc., 375 Hudson Street,
New York, New York 10014, U.S.A.
Penguin Books Ltd, 27 Wrights Lane,
London W8 5TZ, England
Penguin Books Australia Ltd, Ringwood,
Victoria, Australia
Penguin Books Canada Ltd, 2801 John Street,
Markham, Ontario, Canada L3R 1B4
Penguin Books (N.Z.) Ltd, 182-190 Wairau Road,
Auckland 10, New Zealand

Penguin Books Ltd, Registered Offices:
Harmondsworth, Middlesex, England

First published by Signet, an imprint of New American Library, a
division of Penguin Books USA Inc.

First Printing, November, 1990
10 9 8 7 6 5 4 3 2 1

Prologue

Tears flowed at the funeral service for Octavius Bellwood, the eighth Earl of Edgemont. Outside the ancestral chapel, the villagers of Edgemonton huddled together, as much to generate warmth in the January chill as to hear the eulogies. The massive chapel doors had been obligingly opened so that none would miss the words of posthumous praise that the great archbishop would bestow upon their benefactor like so many gold coins on rent day.

"Oh, and ain't it a pity?" murmured the miller's wife to the cobbler's daughter. "And his lordship in the prime of health, to my eyes."

They both shook their heads sadly, two among many doing likewise. As befitting tribute to the gentleman who leased them their land and purchased their goods and services, the villagers gladly conjured up the sufficient emotions, sniffling and mopping their eyes with none-too-clean kerchiefs.

The large staff of Bellwood House, trained to show tribute less profligately, stood stiff and stoic in the back of the chapel, eyes glistening and upper lips trembling, a subdued demonstration of respect with which their late lord and master would have been justly satisfied. In such a setting as the fifteenth-century Gothic chapel, with the brilliant stained-glass windows shimmering in the pale winter sunlight and the goodness of the Almighty via the clergyman's eulogy flowing like wine at a feast, one could conveniently over- look the harshness and irascibility by which the late earl was most well-known. Indeed, judging from the reactions, both blatant and subtle, of those standing in and around the chapel, the late earl would be sorely missed by all.

". . . a gentleman of decided purpose . . ." the honored clergyman intoned, seeming to confirm this deduction.

Curiously, though, in the chapel proper, with seating reserved for family and aristocratic friends prudently bundled in fashionable furs, only one person delicately dabbed at the tears moistening her cheeks.

Felicity Bellwood, niece of the eighth earl, vaguely heard the stentorian words of the archbishop, down from London as a special favor to lay to rest his old friend. She was remembering with fondness the stern uncle who snapped out orders like the crack of a carriage whip, yet answered with blustering pride all her many questions about the vast estate. It was Uncle Octavius who had instilled in her an abiding love of the rolling meadows, the crystalline brooks wriggling with trout, the dark and loamy forest standing as sentinel to their ancestral land.

Perhaps because his own daughter far preferred playing with her dolls to roving the muddy fields, Octavius had lavished his greatest love—that for family pride—on Felicity. She had no illusions that his first choice on which to bequeath such an honor would have been her elder brother, Peter. But Peter had little interest in the matter. Even as a child, on his rare school holidays at Bellwood, he had obediently but impatiently listened to Uncle Octavius' ramblings, anxious to get back to his lead soldiers and war-tactics textbooks.

Felicity now glanced with pride at her beloved brother, so somber in his mourning cloak. His handsome features and military bearing nearly cried out for the enhancement of a uniform. But since the tragedy . . . Felicity averted her eyes from the pain that memory brought full-force.

The other mourners seemed lost in their own thoughts. Aunt Harriet, the widow, whom Felicity could see but in profile, had tilted her chin and compressed her lips in a defense against her loss. Harriet's daughter, Georgina, toyed with a black lace handkerchief to distract herself from the sadness of the moment. Sir Edmund, her uncle's close friend and neighbor, rubbed reflectively at his chin, undoubtedly remembering more joyous times past. And Felicity's father appeared half-dazed, as though he could scarcely believe that his elder brother was indeed gone.

As the archbishop finished his eulogy, the silence itself seemed a tribute to Uncle Octavius. Felicity turned slightly in her pew, raising her veil, noting with pride that the household staff circling the rear of the chapel reflected the family honor in their stance and demeanor.

And then she espied the tall, distinguished stranger standing among them. By the excellent cut of his black superfine cloth coat, the pristine snowiness of his linen, and most especially by the strength of his aristocratic bearing, she knew he was nobody's servant, but perhaps a friend of her uncle's, albeit one whom she had never met. He seemed slightly more advanced in age than her own brother, and in his dark eyes Felicity read a worldliness of which she herself was quite mystified.

For a moment Felicity thought to beckon to him, to invite him to seat himself among family and friends, as befitted his obvious status. But the stranger too seemed preoccupied by his own grief, for he stared forward without seeing, and only a slight furrowing of his brow betrayed his sadness.

Touched, and not a little intrigued, Felicity made a mental note to ask the family about the identity of the man. Then

the thought occurred to her that he would most likely attend
the small luncheon prepared for the guests after the service.
She would be certain to thank him personally for the respect
and honor he had shown Uncle Octavius.

The idea of such devotion brought fresh tears to Felicity's
eyes, and she pressed her handkerchief to her cheeks. This
time her tears sprang from an intense pride and grateful
acknowledgment of the expression of sympathy among the
mourners.

Thus Felicity said her silent farewell to the beloved late
departed, Octavius Bellwood, interpreting the motivations
of everyone present in blissful innocence.

She would have been stunned to her toes to realize that
she was absolutely, horrendously wrong on all counts.

The stranger whom Felicity had noticed had no such
illusions about the principals present.

Justin Havilland, Viscount Pentclair, had chosen his spot
among the servants deliberately. The fury, humiliation, and,
yes, grief that he reined with such fierce determination of
will would be in danger of breaking loose in a devastating
burst of anger should he place himself in such proximity to
the treacherous Bellwood clan.

Were they all aware of the lurid circumstances surrounding Octavius Bellwood's untimely death? Justin had the gut-
wrenching feeling that they must be. Such scandal spread
like flame among tinder, and only by awareness could a
family band together as a firewall against a public blaze of
shame.

The widow, tight-laced and tight-lipped, certainly must
know. The daughter displayed a suspicious nervousness out
of place at a funeral service. The brother, the new earl,
looked more dismayed than distraught. And Peter Bellwood,
the only member of the family whom Justin actually knew

personally, had refused to meet his friend's gaze, his own eyes shadowed by guilt.

The guilt of knowing what happened, Justin thought bitterly.

The one person about whom Justin had his doubts was the young woman seated next to Peter. His wife? Justin mused. Certainly not, for even an avowed rake like Peter Bellwood would have had cause to mention a wife over the course of their mutual adventures. His sister? More likely, although Peter had referred to her only casually, and at that in words that implied she was merely a child.

This woman was no child. From the delicate curve of her back and the slender elegance of her neck, visible through the sheer mourning veil, Justin perceived that she hovered on the brink of beauty. It was difficult indeed to assess her features under the raiment of mourning. But then she shifted in her pew, her gaze scanning the chapel and coming to rest directly upon him.

Justin caught his breath. Framed by the severe black of mourning, her face stood out fetchingly pale, her complexion as soft and delicate as the creamy roses that bloomed in his summer garden. She smiled tentatively at him, and his heartbeat quickened before she slowly turned back to face the front of the chapel.

Fighting for composure, Justin considered that smile. Her lips had curved so unexpectedly, yet so naturally, like a flicker of sunlight through a canopy of clouds. From the unstudied ease of that gesture, he once would have wagered his finest pair of horses that a genuine, innocent motive lay behind that steady gaze.

But now he knew to measure the fair sex differently.

Were not all women natural actresses? Did they not select expressions to wear for every occasion, much as they chose gowns from their modistes? Could they not conjure up a flood of tears, a come-hither laugh, and, indeed, a wistful smile, at the drop of a dressmaker's pin?

Peter's sister, for all her ambience of openness, was the most dangerous Bellwood of all, for her feminine charms fairly begged for the stage and promised an alluring peril to any man so foolish to believe the lie of her innocence.

Justin set his mouth in a determined line. Then and there he vowed to exact his retribution. Somehow his family's honor, unsullied for generations, would be restored. The mantle of responsibility fell upon his broad shoulders, and he would not shrug it off until the Havilland name shone as brightly as ever it had.

Before the service had ended, before he would be confronted by any of the Bellwood clan, Justin Havilland slipped quietly from the chapel. The crowd of villagers stepped respectfully aside, eyeing him curiously, but Justin was not even slightly aware of them. He climbed upon his massive roan gelding and spurred the horse homeward.

His purpose defined, he had but to decide upon the means to polish the tarnished Havilland name. Only fleetingly did the pale and lovely face of Peter Bellwood's sister flash in his mind's eye. As swiftly as it appeared, he banished the vision.

No one's delicate smile would divert him from his crusade.

1

The earth exhibited far more forgiveness than those who trod her ground.

Thus ran Felicity's thoughts some fourteen months later as she passed the family burial plot. Grass had spread soothingly over the cut in the earth where Uncle Octavius had been laid to rest. Even the white marble headstone bore a faint green shadow of moss about the base, evidence of nature's softening effect upon the harsh realities of mankind. Truthful shame to tell, the family of the late earl could not seem to do the same with his memory.

With something of an uncomprehending shrug, Felicity urged her horse into a trot. The long, winding lane leading from Bellwood House to the post road was lined with tall beech forest, the frail new leaves fluttering hopefully in the stiffening spring breeze. She lifted her face toward the trees, oblivious of the gathering clouds overhead.

It was ever so much more hopeful a springtime in general than last year, she mused. So much upheaval, so much confusion . . .

Nearly a month had passed after Uncle Octavius' death before Felicity realized the true import of his demise. Among the most profound of changes was the fact that her father

was now the ninth earl, encumbered with all the duties
thereof. Somewhat reluctantly the household moved from
the charming sixteenth-century dower house to the magnificent seat of the earldom, Bellwood House. A vast, sprawling
mansion, the new residence had served to daunt Felicity, for
officially she now became mistress of the estate. In an ironic
stroke of fortune, the very death that had thrust these new
duties upon her also deemed that a one-year period of official
mourning preclude any entertaining expected of Lord
Augustus Bellwood and his family. Felicity had a year's
reprieve to learn the complex tasks involved in running a
grand country home.

There were so many details to handle. Lists upon lists were
thrust at her for her approval: menus, linens, staff engagings
and dismissals. Daily she thanked heaven for the dour and
formidable Dobbs, majordomo at Bellwood House for nearly
thirty years. This taciturn man attended to the efficiency of
the household, and Felicity prudently decided to allow him
his head in most matters. His attention left her free to pursue
her own interests. And she had not known even how much
she depended on the majordomo until last week, when he
had been forced out of action by an ague. But he was im-
proving, and insisted he would be on his feet in a day or two.

None too soon for Felicity's taste. Even now, at the thought
of her own temporary freedom from the complex business
of running the household, Felicity snapped her heel into
Sheba's side and the feisty little mare speeded up the pace.
With no one's disapproving eyes upon her, she tucked her
riding skirt firmly underneath her limbs and urged the horse
into a light gallop.

Felicity justly took pride in her superb horsemanship,
secretly considering that she held as excellent a seat upon
her mare as any gentleman of her acquaintance, except
perhaps her brother, Peter, before his impediment. And

allowing for the inherent difficulties of balancing precariously upon a sidesaddle, she might, in fact, rate as highly as he.

After a few minutes, though, Felicity reluctantly reined in the mare. There would be no end of recriminations should she arrive to meet Aunt Harriet's coach flushed from her ride. At all costs, she wished to stand firmly on her aunt's approving side.

Perhaps the most difficult adjustment in the past year had been the reversal of roles between Aunt Harriet and her. The widow was undertandably high-strung and out of sorts following the untimely death of her husband, and Felicity did not wish to foment a family crisis by ousting the woman from her home. In fact Felicity gladly would have allowed the dowager countess to remain as mistress of the estate, fond as she was of her opinionated aunt. But curiously, Harriet herself had insisted upon abdicating the role, announcing that they would merely trade residences. With much fervent pleading for need of her aunt's guidance, Felicity had managed to persuade Harriet to remain at Bellwood House, moving only to the east wing. There was certainly room aplenty for all of them. Yet until two months ago, when the official mourning period was done and Harriet had embarked upon a frenetic round of visiting, a strained tension had permeated the household.

For some odd reason, Aunt Harriet seemed almost angry with Uncle Octavius, as if he had offended her by dying so suddenly. Her reaction puzzled Felicity to no end; but Felicity had never did quite understood their ties to one another during her uncle's life. She truly could not decide if Harriet had been happy or miserable with Octavius, for Felicity had observed evidence of both extremes.

But then, Felicity was secretly baffled by all marital webs and ties, and even by the very desire of any woman to marry. In her estimation, the woman involved inevitably got the worse end of the bargain. Her existence became a series of weak reactions to her husband's deeds rather than strong actions of her own. It seemed to Felicity that a wedded woman was forced to play a secondary role in her own life; and she, accustomed to her own relative independence, shuddered at the mere thought of such a restriction. She herself would never desire any manner of husband, and marveled that any woman would.

Yet she knew that at times, Harriet had appeared to be inordinately fond of Octavius, and her aunt was by no stretch of the imagination content to play the weakling. The entire dilemma left Felicity quite puzzled, and Harriet's anger of late only deepened her quandary.

When she mused upon the subject, Felicity had to own that her father and brother also appeared to accept Octavius' passing grudgingly. Indeed, the entire family seemed hard-pressed to forgive her uncle for his death, and for the life of her, she could not understand why.

As she came to the end of the lane and halted to await her aunt's coach, Felicity shooed the perplexing thoughts from her mind. With her eternal optimism, she considered that Aunt Harriet should be in a refreshed mood from her two months' absence. Perhaps now she could cease blaming her late husband for leaving her so abruptly.

Even though the March sky roiled with an approaching storm, Felicity smiled, anticipating Harriet's arrival.

A sinister breeze rustled the young leaves and billowed the black cloak that enveloped the highwayman. He surveyed his handiwork—the felled tree placed as if by random winds across the post road—with guarded satisfaction as the afternoon sky darkened with swift-gathering clouds.

His horse, tethered to a nearby branch, pawed the ground nervously, fatigued from their neck-or-nothing ride. A lone horseman had the advantage of speed by far over a leisurely traveling coach. Yet the highwayman had urged his mount on, to prepare the scene of the holdup.

Now he swung easily onto the great animal's back, murmuring soothing words that lay in stark contrast to the treachery he intended. Abruptly his words faded, as if brushed away by the quickening wind. His ears strained for the sounds he sought. With a grim, determined smile, he pulled his wide-brimmed hat low and tied a black silk kerchief over the bottom half of his face.

The traveling coach, with much rumbling over the rutted road and jangling of harnesses, approached the bend. At the last moment, the coachman, slumped languorously on his perch, bolted upright and pulled on the reins.

"Whoa, there!" he cried in alarm, and the horses stumbled and whinnied in protest, more at the obstruction in their path than at their master's startled command.

"What is it now, Plinn?" a vexatious lady queried from inside the coach.

The highwayman took it upon himself to answer. He spurred his horse forward from behind the sheltering tree and stopped not five yards from the carriage door.

" 'Tis yer destiny," he growled, his Yorkshire accent biting in the wind.

Frozen in surprise, the coachman opened his mouth and stared. The woman inside, however, showed less discretion. Flinging open the carriage door, Lady Harriet Bellwood lowered herself to the ground with much rustling of skirts and dignity.

"What is the meaning of this?" she demanded, facing the highwayman with quivering umbrage.

A handsome woman of a certain age, she bore the straight-backed insistence of one accustomed to having her orders instantly obeyed. The highwayman chuckled.

"I'll have yer jewel case and be on me way, thankee."

"What? You certainly shall not. This is an outrage. I shall report you to the local justice. Be off, you blackguard!"

Slowly the highwayman moved his twin pistols from beneath his cloak into plain sight. With a deliberate motion he cocked the weapons, the menacing click of the hammers unmistakably a threat.

"You do not frighten me," the lady said witheringly.

"Perhaps not," the highwayman countered in affable tones. "Perhaps you've lived a long enough life to face death without fear. But I'll wager yer young daughter, hiding in the coach, might have a ken to live some years longer."

At the mention of her daughter, the lady's indignant composure wavered. She glanced over her shoulder uncertainly. The highwayman chose that precise moment to fire off one of his pistols, aiming toward the sky. All present, except the calm highwayman, jumped in alarm.

Through tight lips, her eyes trained on the highwayman's disguised face, Lady Harriet muttered, "Pass down my jewel case, Georgina."

As though offering him hemlock, Harriet held the case up to the mounted man. He clasped it swiftly, and in a swirl of his cape, wheeled his horse and bolted into the thick woods.

"Oh, yer ladyship," the coachman moaned.

"Stop your blathering, Plinn," she snapped, lifting her skirts in a most unladylike manner to get back into the carriage. "A fine defense of ladies you offer. 'Tis a bare wonder we are not murdered where we stand."

As the import of her words seeped into her mind, she wiped a handkerchief across her perspiring brow.

"Move that tree immediately. And get us to my brother-in-law's as swiftly as you can. That cur of a highpad will pay for what he has done."

As Plinn grunted in his labor, another rider approached suddenly from the opposite side of the road.

"Plinn, is that you?" Felicity cried, maneuvering her mare around the felled tree. "I heard a pistol shot—"

"Felicity!" Lady Harriet called from inside the coach. "Come in here immediately. There is a murderer about!"

"Are you safe, Aunt Harriet? What has happened?"

"We," the woman announced dramatically, "have been robbed by a highpad. In broad daylight, yet! He threatened to kill us and stole our jewels and sped off through the wood. Now, come in here and . . . Fecility!"

Her niece never heard the final command. Without thinking, she reined Sheba about and took off onto the wooded path, her only thought a sense of outrage that a thief should dare to escape through Bellwood land.

A woman of lesser skills would not have progressed more than ten feet without falling, situated in such a delicate balance upon the mare. But Felicity long had possessed startling talent in the saddle, a fact of unladylike expertise that her father and brother judiciously concealed from all and sundry. She goaded Sheba into a full gallop.

Racing as she was down a well-known path, the bushes and trees a green blur streaking on either side of her, Felicity was not surprised soon to espy the highwayman, his black cloak unfurling behind him. Obviously unfamiliar with the path, he was proceeding at a more cautious pace. When he heard the pounding of Sheba's hooves, he turned, startled. Then menacingly he pulled forth his pistol and fired a shot into the treetops.

Sheba whinnied in alarm and shied sharply to the left. Caught by surprise, Felicity had all she could manage to cling desperately to the mare's neck as she felt herself sliding from the sidesaddle. With her foot trapped in the stirrup, and the danger of being trampled to death under Sheba's hooves imminent, Felicity let out a scream of terror.

Branches ripped off her plumed hat and pulled the pins from her hair.

"Sheba, whoa!" she cried, to no avail.

Suddenly the mare skidded to a nervous halt. Through the hammering of her heart, Felicity heard another horse snorting and realized that the highwayman had caught up to her, saving her from certain death. But before she could breathe a relieved sigh, the thought of her peril at his hands caused her to gasp in fright.

She was aware of a swirl of black cloth as he dismounted; then a silk kerchief covered her eyes and was knotted at the back of her head. Still barely daring to breathe, Felicity felt herself roughly lifted upright and seated none too gently upon her mare.

"If ye value yer life," he muttered harshly, "don't be removin' the blind until ye hear no more hoofbeats. I've one shot left, and I won't hesitate to use it. Understand?"

She nodded fearfully as he placed the reins in her trembling hands. Frightened out of her wits, Felicity waited as he had instructed. Distant thunder rolled over the countryside, but soon the pounding of hoofbeats disappeared. She pulled the kerchief from her eyes. Then she headed back toward the post road at only slightly less frantic a pace than she had come from it.

Plinn was finishing the task of removing the fallen tree, which was not much more than a sapling, from the road when she approached.

"Felicity Bellwood!" Aunt Harriet roared. "Have you lost your wits entirely?"

When she saw the tears in Felicity's riding habit and her tangled pale auburn tresses, Lady Harriet's outrage turned to alarmed concern.

"Has that blackguard harmed you? Oh, my dearest—"

"No, Aunt Harriet," Felicity murmured, trembling the more at the realization of her folly. "I nearly slipped from Sheba's back."

"Oh, the idiocy of a lady riding upon a beast!" Harriet moaned. "Come inside this coach immediately, and ride like a civilized person. Plinn, help her down and tie that animal off behind."

Grateful for Plinn's sturdy arms, Felicity allowed him to assist her. None too steadily, she climbed into the coach.

Aunt Harriet began her tirade even before the carriage began rolling.

"I cannot credit the frame of mind that would allow you to behave so rashly. Certainly not in the manner of the daughter of an earl! This incident only reaffirms my notion in returning to Bellwood House. 'Tis long past time for drastic changes, Felicity. That vile highwayman's robbing us of our jewels, not to mention your ridiculously foolish pursuit of that man, to what end I cannot even imagine, is proof."

She paused merely to catch her breath, nodding in her most straight-lipped determination.

"First, a glass of your father's best brandy. Then I shall tell you exactly what those drastic changes must encompass."

Felicity remained silent. She had an uneasy feeling that the audacious highwayman had wreaked more havoc than he would ever know.

2

Felicity, still shaken from her encounter, huddled in a corner of the traveling coach, absently combing her fingers through her long gold-red hair. Bits of leaves and twigs fluttered to her lap, but she did not notice. She listened only to every tenth word of her aunt's recriminations, although she glanced up now and again to measure Lady Harriet's expression.

Still on the near side of forty, but uncomfortably close, Lady Harriet had proved herself expert in preserving her beauty. Since her husband's death, much of the gleam had dimmed in her dark eyes and hair, and, indeed, in her spirit. But ironically, the highwayman had restored a modicum of her spark. Gratified to see her aunt acting more herself, Felicity only prayed that she herself would not be found too far outside her aunt's favor.

Lady Harriet ranted on until Plinn halted the traveling coach before the great doors of Bellwood House. Sensing that silence was the better part of valor, considering her aunt's mood, Felicity said not a word until the footmen had helped them from the coach. Then, while Aunt Harriet gave the servants strict orders regarding her trunks, Felicity motioned the coachman aside.

"Plinn, when you take the coach around, please see that McCafferty himself takes charge of Sheba. She must be cooled and brushed with especial care."

"Aye, miss."

She followed her aunt into the petite foyer, where they were met by the head footman.

"Where is Dobbs?" Harriet demanded.

"I fear he has taken ill, aunt," Felicity answered. "But he will return to his duties in a few days."

"Is there a fire laid in the receiving room?" Aunt Harriet asked the head footman as he took her hat and gloves.

If the servant took note of Felicity's missing hat, the small rips in her garments, and her wildly disheveled hair, his strict training kept his expression impassive. "Yes, milady. May I bring you some refreshment?"

"The prewar brandy. And three glasses. No, four. Ask Sir Augustus to join us immediately."

The head footman shook his head dubiously. "His lordship is at the stables as usual, milady. He has given us orders not to disturb—"

"Distrub him," Harriet snapped. "The matter is urgent."

Allowing himself a brief glance at Felicity's appearance, the head footman murmured, "Indeed, milady," and left to do her bidding.

Aunt Harriet started off toward the receiving room, but Felicity hesitated.

"Aunt, I should like to freshen up, if you would excuse me for—"

"Indeed I shall not," Harriet called over her shoulder. "I want your father to see precisely what his deeds have wrought."

"His deeds? Surely you do not suppose that Papa has any inkling about that highwayman."

"Certainly not. But he should have."

Failing to track her aunt's logic, Felicity frowned but followed obediently.

"Georgina, you come along also. And kindly cease your dawdling. 'Tis most unlike you."

Until Harriet fired off the command to her daughter, Felicity had nearly forgotten that Georgina was with them, so quiet was her cousin. And Georgina was indeed behaving in a manner most unlike her usual effervescent self.

Felicity gave her a puzzled but encouraging smile, and to her astonishment, Georgina's heart-shaped face almost crumpled into tears. Taking her cousin's arm, Felicity whispered, "Georgina, dear, what is it?"

Georgina shot her a glance near to wild in its dismay and shook off Felicity's arm.

Dropping a pace behind her relentlessly striding aunt and her nervously scurrying cousin, Felicity considered the response. How callous of her! Naturally, Georgina would be distraught by the incident on the post road. Highwaymen were not supposed to be a danger these days, having for the most part gone the way of powdered wigs and panniers, owing to the more voluminous traffic on the roads. Ladies presumed themselves quite safe while traveling, with the normal precaution of a capable coachman to convey them to their destinations. What a blow to be accosted so!

Now that she mused upon the subject, Felicity had to own that the more astonishing reaction had been hers. Whatever had possessed her to go hurtling off after that man? For all she knew, he might well have been a cutthroat to boot, willing to slash her neck for the prize of her horse, or even merely for the sake of protecting his identity. Her father might well have ridden after the thief; her brother, Peter, certainly would have. But she?

A chill prickled at her nape and Felicity felt distinctly faint. She paused for a moment to regain her bearings.

Bellwood House, as most other grand country estates, could trace its origins many centuries back. And also like most homes of its ilk, succeeding generations had added wings as the need arose. The petite foyer jutted out from the rest of the manor, constructed a mere two hundred years ago to lead into a massive room in the oldest portion of the house, a room that in medieval times was called the great hall.

As she paused, Felicity felt the eyes of the many ancestral portraits boring into her. Today had proved that she was falling far short of the role demanded of the lady of the manor. She even imagined the raised eyebrows of the horrified former mistresses of the estate. As one who actually delved into the library of extensive journals kept by these ladies of history, she knew that they had concerned themselves with their proper roles in the household. Felicity, the latest in their proud and noble line, was in danger of proving herself a true hoyden. She shuddered at the potential black mark upon the family honor.

"Felicity!"

"Coming, aunt." To Felicity's chagrin, her voice trembled slightly, as if in guilt.

The drawing room, far more cozy by its relatively diminutive size than the more formal grand parlor, emitted a cheery warmth as they entered. True to the head footman's word, a robust fire blazed on the hearth. Despite its glow, the threatening skies had rendered the room as dark as if it were evening, and the downstairs maids, obviously alerted by the footmen, hurried about now lighting the lamps as the storm finally broke. They glanced wide-eyed at Felicity's tousled appearance, and although she remained outwardly composed, Felicity resigned herself to the certainty of being the subject of wild speculation in the servants' wing. Another black mark against her.

"Come up to the fire, the both of you," Aunt Harriet

ordered. "I shall not add to this disaster by having either
of you catching your death of a chill."

Felicity and Georgina complied, and Felicity had to admit
that the warmth chased away a bit of the cold dread that had
filled her.

"Good for the outside," Harriet decided, shooing them
both to nearby chairs as Dobbs arrived with the restorative.
"Now for the inside."

She poured them each a small splash of brandy. Felicity
had never imbibed a spirit stronger than wine, and the first
taste flamed down the length of her throat. She coughed
loudly.

"For mercy's sake, Felicity," Aunt Harriet grumbled.
"One does not gulp brandy like water. One sips. Slowly."

With the expertise Aunt Harriet exhibited, Felicity had
cause to wonder how very well-acquainted the woman was
with the drink. Dismissing the thought as unworthy and
mean, she reminded herself of the medicinal purposes of this
particular instance. When she took her aunt's advice and
sipped, the brandy indeed did seem more to warm than to
burn.

Just as Felicity was beginning to regain her strength, the
doors to the drawing room burst open, startling them all.

"I say, Harriet," Augustus Bellwood blustered as he
stormed in, "what is so damned urgent that you must—"

He halted mid-tirade as he espied his daughter.

"Felicity! My God, what has happened? Are you hurt?"

Rushing to her side, he alternately crushed her in his
embrace and pulled away to gaze anxiously at her.

"I am very well, Papa," Felicity assured him.

"No more to your credit, Augustus," Harriet added tartly.

Augustus turned to her. "Why does my daughter look as
if she's plunged through a hedgerow? What the devil has
happened?"

Rising majestically to her feet, Harriet replied, "You may rave all you like, brother-in-law, but I shall not abide your cursing before ladies. Once more, and we shall retire to our quarters and you may whistle for your explanations!"

"By God, madam . . . Wait, wait! I beg your forgiveness. But surely you understand how distressing it is to find one's daughter in such a state. Please. I vow I shall bite my tongue before I curse in the presence of ladies again."

Spending as much time in the stables as she had, Felicity was far from offended by his mild oaths. She had heard worse from his mouth when a horse shied at taking the bit. Nonetheless, she smiled fondly at her father's promise to curb his tongue.

Pausing to judge the depth of his sincerity, Harriet finally nodded in satisfaction and seated herself once more. When Augustus' tension was palpable in the room, she informed him placidly, "Georgina and I have been robbed of our jewels by a highwayman."

"What! By dam . . . er, by Jove, you say. A highpad! In this part of the county?"

Harriet smiled icily. "One would presume. He came from and escaped over Bellwood land."

Augustus slammed his fist into his open palm. "The cheek of the fellow! I shall hunt him down like the devious fox he is."

"Restrain yourself, Augustus," Harriet answered dryly. "By now he is halfway to London to cash in on his luck. Have a brandy and calm yourself."

As her father willingly obliged Harriet, swallowing one and then another gulp for good measure, Felicity glanced at him from under lowered lashes. Until now she had remained gladly silent, happy that his ire was being vented upon the highwayman. When he learned of her part in the drama, he undoubtedly would target her.

Augustus Bellwood, like all the Bellwood men, was tall and powerful, with thick hair nearly the color of mahogany wood. He was an uncomplicated man, and his moods were easily gauged by his expression, much as one could read the weather merely by gazing at the sky. When he was peeved, he blustered noisily. When content, he sang under his breath. He could switch from a murmur to a shout in mid-sentence. But because he was naturally more contented than not, his fits of temper blazed and then sputtered, swift-running fuses that burned themselves out and promptly were forgotten.

Felicity never had feared her father's wrath. She knew it for what it was, a display of anxiety or annoyance or even affection, and she normally could distinguish among the choices to supply the fitting motivation. The only reaction she dreaded from him, and dreaded more than the Black Death, was his disappointment in her. On the extremely rare occasions when she had realized that this was the stimulus for his temper, she had cringed in regret.

Her one hope now was that Augustus, truly angered by the gall of the highwayman, would exhaust his ire venting it upon the robber, having none left to turn on her. To that end, she sank lower in her chair, attempting to make herself as unobtrusive as possible.

Indeed, Augustus still focused on the robbery.

"A highwayman on Bellwood land," he muttered, as if to convince himself of such an astonishing occurrence.

"Yes, Augustus," Harriet said calmly. "And one may lay the blame entirely at your feet."

"At my feet! The dev . . ." The deuce you say, madam!"

"Careful, Augustus," Harriet warned. "I understand euphemisms as well as the next, and you are decidedly close to offending me."

His face reddening in frustration, Augustus almost literally bit his tongue. From past experience, Felicity knew how he longed to spew forth a stream of satisfying curses. She could not help admiring the uncustomary restraint he exercised.

Taking a deep breath, he began again. "How can you lay the blame for this blackguard's deed at my feet?"

Harriet sipped delicately at her brandy. "You obviously are neglecting your duties as master of this estate."

Firing that particular fusillade, Felicity knew, was a decided blunder. To confirm her judgment, Augustus turned stiffly to his sister-in-law.

"I beg your pardon, madam, but you seem to forget that I *am* master of this estate and, therefore, my duties are precisely as I define them."

Harriet would not desist. "You turn your attention solely to the stables."

"And Bellwood stock has never thrived as it has under my hands," Augustus retorted with, in Felicity's mind, justifiable pride. "Our reputation is excellent throughout England, indeed, wherever fine horesflesh is prized."

Waving away his claim as if it were irrelevant, Harriet said, "But what of your duties in Parliament, Augustus? I spoke to the Prince Regent only a fortnight ago, and he asked most pointedly about your well-known absences from the House."

At that remark, Augustus surprisingly grinned. "I am better-acquainted with our Prinny than you, madam. Credit me when I say that he far prefers my breeding a good racing stock to my meddling in political affairs."

Felicity hid a smile, for Harriet plainly realized that Augustus spoke the truth and had scored an important point. Nevertheless, she persisted.

"Then hide yourself in the country if you must. I still vow that you are lax in your duties here also. Were you attending to the affairs of the estate, no highwayman would dare escort us in broad daylight and demand our jewels."

Now that she had retreated once, Augustus' eyes shone

with a perceptive glimmer and he went on the offensive.

"Speaking of which, Harriet," he said slyly, "I find it curious that you seem more distraught that a highpad ventured forth on Bellwood property than that he stole your trinkets. Dam . . . er, decidedly curious."

Smugly she gazed upon him. "Unwittingly, you have chosen the correct word. 'Trinkets' are precisely what that cur stole."

All eyes blinked at her.

"But, Aunt Harriet," Felicity blurted, forgetting her vow to fade into the background, "Great-Grandmama's pearls. The Queen Mary tiara. Surely those pieces cannot be deemed mere trinkets."

"No, indeed," Harriet replied grimly. "Which is precisely why I always pack them in the bottom drawer of my most hefty trunk. They are now safely in my chambers, being carefully unpacked, I presume, by my maid. Thank the heavens I sent her on ahead. The sight of that highpad would have plunged her into a month-long attack of the vapors."

Augustus frowned and pulled at his chin. "The bottom of your trunk. I never have heard of such. One carries jewels in a jewel case."

Fixing him with a scathing look, Harriet said, "How very brilliant, Augustus. Should I have agreed with that popular theory, the Bellwood jewels would now be in the filthy hands of some East End broker. I take my responsibility seriously. When Peter weds, I shall hand those pieces to his wife in good conscience, having preserved the family legacy."

"Oh, Aunt Harriet," Felicity sighed. "I am so relieved. And is it not astonishing good luck that you placed those jewels so? Almost as if you had a premonition that they should be safer in the trunk."

Harriet snorted. "It was no premonition." For the briefest moment her composure faltered and Felicity thought that she seemed uneasy. "There were those about whom I have had suspicions. Treachery dwells in the most unlikely hearts."

"That is precisely the reason I am loath to leave the confines of the estate," Augustus announced, triumphantly scoring another point. "Bellwood servants are as trustworthy as the earth beneath one's feet. But other households are not as careful about whom they employ."

Pausing a moment, Harriet then shrugged. But Felicity sensed that servants were not the source of her aunt's concern. Before she could ponder the idea further, Georgina suddenly and surprisingly burst into tears.

Instinctively Felicity moved to encircle her cousin with a comforting arm. "Georgina, dear, what is it?"

Unnerved by feminine tears, Augustus turned brisk. "Here, here, miss. No harm done, so all's well." When Georgina did not cease in her sobbing, Augustus focused belatedly on his daughter.

"And you, Felicity, still have not given me a proper explanation. Why is your hair all tumbled about?"

"Never mind her tresses," Harriet said peevishly. "Georgina, do stop that caterwauling. The incident is done, and we survived quite nicely. Not that that fact mitigates your Uncle Augustus' responsibility."

Noting that her father and aunt were about to set to once more, Felicity hastily intervened.

"Georgina, do dry your eyes. Are you feeling unwell? Would you like to retire to your chamber?"

Georgina nodded eagerly, her eyes glistening with hope, but Harriet would have one of it.

"Nonsense. Georgina, you will stay put until you tell me exactly what is causing this font of tears. You have been behaving most strangely since the day I collected you at your town house. I have raised you to be steady and sensible, and until now, I assumed I had succeeded. But here you are, a grown woman, and emoting like a dim-witted actress for a week's time. My patience is thinning to the point of non-existence."

Georgina, delicate as a porcelain doll, shook her dark ringlets vehemently. "I . . . I cannot tell you, Mama."

"And why not, may I ask?"

"Because you will undoubtedly disown me."

When a new round of wailing threatened to burst forth from Georgina, Harriet motioned for Felicity to give the girl another sip of brandy. With soothing urges, Felicity managed to get a drop past her cousin's lips.

Harriet smiled tightly. "The only justification I might find to disown you, dear daughter, is that you refuse to tell me what on earth is causing this hysteria."

Sighing deeply, with a look of doom on her pretty face, Georgina relented. "Last evening, as we visited the Blemfields, you were fatigued and retired early."

When she hesitated, Harriet nodded impatiently. "Yes, yes, my mind is still capable of stretching back twenty or so hours. Go on."

"Well, Jane and I were bored, and she asked to see the Bellwood ruby set, which she had heard praised so highly. We looked through your jewel case and found only a few minor pieces. Silver earbobs, a malachite fob, an onyx bracelet that I don't even remember your having."

Harriet's lips tightened. " 'Twas a gift from Octavius."

"Oh, Mama, I am sorry. How awful for you to lose that piece!"

Upon first glance, Felicity too might have interpreted her aunt's response as one of regret. But apparently she alone had heard the inflection on the word "gift." By the tone of her voice, Harriet might well have said "poison."

Before she could ponder the strange reply further, Harriet said, "Go on, Georgina."

"Oh, dear. Well, Grendall was preparing your trunks for the next day, and was flustered about leaving before us at first light. She showed me the drawer with your truly magnificent pieces and Jane and I had a lovely hour admiring them. But then Grendall became vexed and shooed us away, that she might finish her tasks. Honestly, Mama, I realize that woman has been your maid for years, but she is becoming quite impudent in her dotage."

"Do not digress, Georgina. Finish your tale."

Georgina twisted her fingers in her lap. "Well, Mama, in the confusion to pack the trunk, one piece was left out. Rather than listen to Grendall's grumbling, I told her . . . I told her to never mind about opening the trunk again. I would put the piece in your small jewel case." Her voice trailed off nearly to silence. "And that is what I did."

Harriet closed her eyes, as if gathering strength to withstand the blow. "Which piece was it?"

Her expression crumpling, Georgina blurted out, "The Cleopatra armlet!"

Involuntarily Felicity gasped. The Cleopatra armlet was one of the most unusual and prized of Bellwood jewels. Designed to be worn above the elbow, the armlet, in the sinuous shape of an asp, was made of emeralds interspersed with diamonds, with twin ruby eyes. Beyond its obvious worth was a special charm. Legend had it that many a Bellwood wife had rekindled her husband's affections while wearing this exotic decoration. Gems could be replaced; charm could not. This turn of events truly was a disaster.

"Oh, Mama," Georgina moaned through her sobs, "I truly think . . . that an evil spell has been cast upon me!"

Sighing heavily, Harriet murmured, "I have reached the far side of enough, coping with your dramatics, Georgina. What's done is done. The situation could be worse. We might have lost the Bellwood rubies."

When Georgina did not reply, Harriet said sharply, "We did not lose the rubies, did we?"

"Oh, no," Georgina hastened to assure her. "No, indeed. They are locked in the trunk, in their special case."

Rising and gathering her dignity about her like a protective cape, Harriet said, "I shall not rest easy until I see them with my own eyes. Come, Georgina."

After her daughter had followed Harriet meekly from the room, Augustus let out a hoot and rubbed his hands together in glee.

"Ha! Well, so much for her great sense of responsibility for the family gems. Now we shall see if the woman has the cheek to chide me about my duties. This should clamp her mouth for years. By damn, I should have that highpad dubbed a knight of the realm!"

"Papa!" Felicity said reprovingly. "How can you be so glib about the Cleopatra armlet? It has been in the family since the Crusades."

Augustus shrugged. "Baubles and gewgaws. What if the Bellwood women sparkle a little less brightly at their balls? Will the family be diminished? I think not. Now, if Emperor should turn up missing . . ."

A horrified frown crossed his face at the very thought of his prize stallion being stolen. "I shall this very minute post guards about the stables and paddocks. When thievery is in the air, there is no predicting where it will strike next."

He turned to go, and Felicity felt the glimmer of a reprieve, grateful that the horses might save her from his disappointment. But at the door he turned back to her.

"Here, here, miss. I never received an explanation for your dishevelment. I am your father, and I demand to know the meaning of this."

Felicity closed her eyes for a moment, then gazed directly and firmly at him.

"I arrived at Aunt Harriet's coach just after the highwayman had vanished into the wood. I . . . I then rode off after him, and I vow, I do not know what I would have done should I have caught up with the man."

"Are you mad, daughter? When I imagine what might have occurred . . . Have you lost your wits?"

"I own that I did not think, Papa. It twas more of an instant reaction, so incensed was I that he had used Bellwood land to make his escape."

"And how did you come to lose your hat and hair pinnings?"

Felicity knew she must proceed cautiously from this point. Until now, Augustus' tone was gruff, but not unbearable. She decided that prudence called for a selection of facts.

"Sheba shied, and I slipped from the saddle. The bushes claimed my hat and, I fear, ruined my riding habit."

She brightened with forced cheer. "But as you see, I am fit and perfectly well."

"Hmph." Augustus peered at her sternly; then a smile twitched at his mouth. "Kept your seat upon the horse, did you, Lissie?"

The use of her childhood name melted Felicity's nerve. She gulped as she replied, "I did not fall off my mare, Papa."

Augustus grinned hugely. "By damn. By damn, I ever knew that you were as fine a rider as any man in the family! Good show, Lissie."

Halfway through the door, he poked his head back inside.

"But, er, were I you, Felicity, I should keep this between us. Your estimable aunt would not consider your skill a virtue, more the fool she. Agreed?"

Nodding eagerly, Felicity answered, "Agreed."

As the door closed, she collapsed against the back of the chair with a profound sigh. Guilt pricked at her that she had omitted the more pertinent facts of her tale. But, she justified, since no harm had befallen her, there was no need to worry her father any further.

As she rose to go dress for dinner, Felicity felt a buoyancy in her step. She had avoided her father's disappointment, one grand surprise among many on this astonishing day.

Unbeknownst to her, larger surprises awaited.

3

Nanny Parker grumbled noisily as she pulled the silver-backed brush through Felicity's tangled curls.

"Whatever was ye thinkin' of, miss? Like to break yer neck, you was, boltin' off like that. I thought I raised ye up better than that, I did, and yerself makin' the liar of me."

Wincing as Nanny tugged at her hair, Felicity kept her peace. The elderly woman had earned her asperity with years of loyal service, beginning when she was a mere slip of a girl herself, charged with the care of Augustus and his siblings. Two generations of Bellwoods had thrived under her capable hands, and since Felicity's mother had succumbed to childbed fever just after her birth, Nanny Parker had comforted and scolded, taught and reproved her. With no other children forthcoming, Nanny's duties slowly evolved into those of a crotchety abigail for Felicity.

That Nanny knew of her escapade this day did not astound Felicity. As a child, she had suspected that the woman's slightly hooked nose and small piercing eyes confirmed her notion that Nanny might be a sorceress, for all her powers of divining what should have been secrets. But the hands that even then were beginning to gnarl caressed too gently to belong to a sorceress. And as Felicity grew older, she realized that the eyes of the servant were the eyes of all, for in the staff quarters they discussed the family more vigorously and held them to higher standards than the family did itself.

And thus Felicity allowed the old woman to voice her disapproval, knowing that beneath the vexation lay a deep pool of tenderness for her.

But now, as Nanny brushed the more harshly, Felicity let forth a tiny squeal. "If you please, Nanny, I should like to have more hair upon my head than in the bristles."

"A detail ye might have remembered before ye scuttled off hither and yon through the wood," Nanny muttered.

Felicity shrugged a concession. In all, she felt revived. A soothing hot soak in a bath scented with lavender oils had accomplished much in the way of calming her and restoring her spirit.

"I think that will do, Nanny," she said, gazing into the hand mirror and noting that her hair shone smooth again. "Pin it up and then bring my gown, if you please."

Sighing mightily, Nanny muttered, "For all the good it does speakin' to ye, I may as well hoard me words. Lord knows I haven't many left."

"Enough of that nonsense," Felicity replied sternly. "You will surely outlive us all, for you could not bear the thought of being unable to chide me."

"When ye do naught to be chided for, I'll stop." She twisted and wound Felicity's hair into a gleaming knot, jabbing in pins recklessly. "Now, stand up and lift yer arms for the gown."

Having learned long ago that one did not fire the last volley against Nanny, Felicity held her tongue and complied. But as the column of silk slipped over her shoulders, Felicity frowned, puzzled.

"Nanny," she said, her voice muffled by the folds of cloth, "this gown will not do."

Undeterred, Nanny settled the ice-blue silk and began to fasten the tiny back buttons, her bent fingers laboring at the task. She had chosen a gown that Aunt Harriet had had commissioned for Felicity two years past upon the occasion of a pre-wedding celebration for Georgina.

"This is much too elegant a gown for a family dinner," Felicity protested.

Persistently Nanny concentrated on the fastening, grunting in triumph when the last button had succumbed to her fingers. "No sense in keepin' it in a trunk till the poor thing goes out of fashion."

"But I do not think—"

"And that, miss, is all the trouble. Ye failed to think, ye did, before ye went off through the wood. And ye aren't thinkin' now. Lord above, if I haven't wasted me time raisin' a witless chit. 'Tisn't just yer old nanny who's cross with ye, I'll wager. It seems to me that his lordship must be fair addled, he must, at the idea of what harm could've come to ye. But lookin' so lovely in that gown, his lordship won't be apt to take on after ye, now will he? Deceive him into thinkin' his daughter's all the lady, ye will."

Felicity hesitated, considering. "This afternoon he did upbraid me in no uncertain terms. But Papa is not one to hold with anger longer than it takes to burn out. Do you suppose that he remains cross with me still?"

"Hmph. As me old mum was wont to say when me fingers got too careless with the candlestick, 'An instant of flame, an hour of pain.' "

Frowning uncertainly, Felicity mused upon her words. The incident of the robbery being of major importance, in all likelihood it would be the subject of much discussion at dinner. Perhaps a charming appearance would overshadow her disgraceful pursuit of the highwayman. But could she present such an image? Filled with secret doubts, she remained silent.

Nanny brought her jewel box, far more modest than Aunt Harriet's cache. Felicity's fingers went first for a lovely cameo brooch.

"Nay, not that," Nanny said decisively. "The color's wrong for this gown."

Felicity released the brooch, reluctantly owning to herself that the unusual green background did clash with the blue of her gown. But she loved the cameo, with its creamy woman's head in a classical hair dressing and patrician pose. By Bellwood standards, it was not an important piece, but Felicity treasured it above any ruby or emerald. It was the first, and only, bit of jewelry Peter had given her. Nonetheless, she offered no protest as Nanny slipped a diamond pendant around her neck and matching bobs in her ears.

Then Nanny pulled a folded handkerchief from the pocket of her voluminous skirt. Carefully she unwrapped the cloth to reveal a bunch of violets.

"Where did you find those?" Felicity asked, amazed.

Nanny feigned nonchalance. "I happened upon 'em whilst strolling about the garden, and it came to me that they would look fetchin', they would, tucked into yer hair."

When Felicity raised her brow in astonishment, Nanny frowned stubbornly. "These old bones ain't failed me yet, they ain't. I do betimes fancy a stroll in the garden."

Felicity recognized the blatant lie. Nanny's rheumatism yearned more for the comfort of a cozy fire than the dampness of a spring garden. Touched by her devotion, Felicity nonetheless murmured only a polite "How lovely." Nanny's insistence upon a gruff demeanor would not permit more effusive affection.

The old woman grimaced in concentration as she tied the violets into two bunches with blue silk ribbons. Then, as she fastened them on either side of Felicity's chignon, a bell tinkled softly in the hallway.

"Right we are," Nanny said briskly, admiring her work.

"Dinner in a quarter hour's time, and apt to deceive the Prince himself into believin' ye're a lady, ye are. Off ye go."

She began to shoo Felicity from the room, mumbling about the troubles caused by headstrong and witless young girls. Felicity dawdled, glancing at herself in the pier glass. The ribbons enhanced the summer blue of her eyes, and in the dinner candlelight, the thin scratch on her cheek—a souvenir of the grasping branches that had clutched at her as she had nearly fallen off her mount—would scarcely be noticeable. Perhaps her appearance in the elegant gown would overshadow her shortcomings and render her almost lovely.

"Come, now," Nanny urged her. "No sense in arriving late to dinner, is there, when ye're wanting to get in his lordship's favor? Off ye go."

Pausing only to snatch up a creamy Kashmir shawl, Felicity allowed herself to be chased downstairs.

When she espied Aunt Harriet and Georgina in the drawing room, waiting to go in to dinner, Felicity silently thanked Nanny for urging her into the smart dress. Out of half-mourning's gray and mauve shades now, both her aunt and her cousin wore gowns *très à la mode*, Harriet in a deep ocher, Georgina in sea-green. While not in formal attire, her father had conceded to his valet's ministrations and looked quite handsome in his superfine coat and neatly tied cravat.

"There you are, Felicity," Lady Harriet proclaimed. She paused, allowing her gaze to measure her niece's appearance. Then, nodding, as if confirming some private thought, she added, "You are capable of looking quite charming when you choose to do so."

"Thank you, aunt," Felicity murmured, unsure of whether or not to be complimented.

"Now, let us go in to dinner. Augustus?"

Her father obligingly, if stiffly, offered Harriet his arm, and the two girls followed them into the dining salon. When her aunt took the chair at the end of the table, the place of honor usually reserved for the lady of the manor, Felicity did not object. Perhaps Harriet, in her none-too-subtle manner, wished to step back into the role, serving as the Bellwood House hostess. If so, Felicity would but rejoice, a hefty burden having been lifted from her own young shoulders.

During the arrival of the footmen bearing steaming silver platters and porcelain terrines, Harriet suddenly caught her breath. With thumb and forefinger she picked up her fork as if holding on to the tail of a dead mouse.

"There is a spot of tarnish on this utensil."

The head footman rushed to her side and took hold of the offending fork in like manner. "My abject apologies, your ladyship."

With a put-upon sniff, Harriet watched as he provided a replacement. Then she inclined her head slightly. "You may now serve."

Silence engulfed the salon as the head footman, in one more of the duties Dobbs usually handled, ladled out the first course of oxtail broth. Felicity trained her gaze upon her plate, knowing that a reprimand was surely forthcoming. Indeed, before she brought the first spoonful to her mouth, Harriet could bide no longer.

"Gracious, Felicity," she murmured so that the servants awaiting her pleasure along the perimeter of the salon could not hear. "Whatever has claimed your time during my absence? Certainly not the management of the staff. This silver has not been polished properly, there is a wine stain on my napery, and the buckle of the third footman's shoe is broken. In the stead of riding, which in my opinion is an unwholesome occupation for any woman, you should have been attending to the household."

Felicity's cheeks reddened as her aunt reinforced the same

sense of disgrace she had felt under the reproving eyes of the portraits in the grand salon.

"Please forgive me, aunt," she replied meekly. "I vow I shall improve."

Oh, if her aunt but knew. Felicity realized she would be stunned by her niece's shortcomings. Felicity had absolutely no interest in household matters. Her father did not mind; indeed, so long as his belly was satisfied, he cared naught whether he ate from bone china or chipped crockery. And, Felicity reasoned, if Augustus did not even notice, why should she devote her days to perfecting skills she would never need? Of course, Aunt Harriet would never understand such logic. Indeed, she would be horrified were she to recognize the true bent of her niece's mind. For of all Felicity's radical ideas, none would flabbergast Harriet more than the understanding that Felicity had no use for what was the very foundation of Harriet's life: making a brilliant marital match.

She had not found the courage to vocalize her decision never to marry. Fortunately, the subject had never arisen, what with Harriet's campaign to see Georgina successfully wedded occupying her time, and then with Octavius' death. But Felicity secretly was determined. She enjoyed her life in the country and would be content to live out her days caring for her father on the estate.

"I shall have to have a long talk with you, Felicity," Aunt Harriet muttered now, and Felicity stifled her groan.

Augustus' voice boomed from the opposite end of the table. "Here, here. What are you two mumbling about?"

"Nothing that concerns you," Harriet answered smoothly. "Household matters."

"Household matters? A topic completely unsuitable at table."

"For once, Augustus, I agree with you. We shall speak of it later."

She fixed her niece with a significant look, and Felicity lowered her gaze nervously. Her aunt was nearer to unmasking her secret than anyone ever had been. Pondering how she would manage to get through this evening, attempting to dodge her father's wrath and her aunt's annoyance, Felicity found that her usually brisk appetite had quite fled away.

Just as she decided to develop a sudden illness to afford her an excuse from the dinner, luck intervened. The door to the dining salon burst open and a broadly grinning young man entered.

"Peter!" Felicity cried, as much in relief as in delight.

"Good evening, dear sister," he replied heartily.

His cheerful mood gratified Felicity no end. She had been much troubled by the determined gloom that so often surrounded her brother of late. But tonight one scarcely noted the limp that had seemed so pronounced when last she had seen him, and a glow emanated through him from his cap of artfully tousled red-gold curls to the toes of his shiny Hessians. Yet her happiness faltered slightly as he came to fix an enthusiastic kiss upon her cheek, for upon his breath she smelled the distinct odor of port wine.

"Aunt Harriet," Peter continued, going round the table. "How ravishing you look. And, Georgina, I vow you grow more fetching by the day. Father. How very good to see you, sir. I hear we have a certain champion for the race meeting upcoming."

They all stared at him, for this was an effusive Peter the likes of which none had glimpsed for years. Harriet recovered first.

"How lovely to see you, nephew. Will you dine with us?"

"Oh, indeed I will," he replied even as the footmen laid

a place for him. "But another placement will be needed. I've brought a guest."

Belatedly Felicity looked again to the doorway. Slowly Peter's guest came forward.

4

The intensity of his presence struck her first. His shoulders so impossibly broad, his bearing unaffectedly proud, he commanded attention without having spoken a word. Quite forgetting her manners, Felicity stared at him in fascination. Did there exist a shade in a paintbox deep enough to capture the dark softness of his hair? Ws there in this world a clay smooth enough to mold a replica of his strong classical features? Her interest focused upon him, she hadn't time to glance away before she realized that her brother was introducing them.

". . . and my sister, Felicity. May I present Justin Havilland, Viscount Pentclair."

As he turned his gaze upon her, Felicity started. The contact of those ebony eyes struck a spark of recognition. She had seen him somewhere before, and yet she could not place him. But surely she would not forget such a memorable man.

"I'm delighted to make your acquaintance, Lady Felicity," he said politely. Yet somehow the declaration did not match his gaze.

Somewhat to her surprise, Felicity detected a wariness and even a slight sadness in his eyes. Suddenly memory returned with a startling clarity. Justin Havilland was the man she had seen at Uncle Octavius' funeral.

Quietly disappointed when he had not appeared after the service, she had dismissed her curiosity when other, pressing matters had required her attention. And now, fourteen months later, he had reappeared in the dining salon as abruptly as he had vanished from the chapel.

Felicity wondered if she should be annoyed with him.

"I pray you will forgive this interruption of your dinner, Sir Augustus," Havilland said now, his smile courteous but by no means apologetic.

"Nonsense, my boy," her father protested. "We are delighted to have you here. Traveled down from London with Peter, did you?"

"No, Sir Augustus. We chanced to meet at an inn where we both were resting our mounts an waiting out the storm."

"And refreshing ourselves," Peter added with a grin, seating himself and immediately motioning for a footman to fill his glass brimful of wine, should anyone have missed the point. "Havilland is looking for horses for his private stable. I persuaded him to come along home with me, trying to convince him that he could do no better than to purchase Bellwood stock."

Havilland shrugged noncommittally.

"My son is immodest, but correct," Augustus allowed. "I should like to show you our finest specimens. One glimpse will no doubt be all the convincing you shall require."

Havilland hesitated, then nodded courteously. "Sir Augustus, I shall consider your proposal."

"Splendid, my boy! You know, in times past I have supplied your family with their mounts and carriage horses. Your esteemed father was most favorably impressed, if I do say so myself. By the by, how is the old fellow? Missed him last year during the grouse hunting."

Havilland's mannerly interest hardened, confirming Felicity's recollection of the near-glower she had glimpsed on that cold January morning.

"He did not leave London. Our family was in mourning."

As the footman held back his chair, Justin Havilland seated himself, and an uneasy silence intruded in the room. Felicity glanced in confusion from their guest to her brother, and then around at the remainder of her family. All save Georgina, who was definitely preoccupied of late and seemed unaware of the entire exchange, wore masks of forced composure. Bewildered, Felicity shivered, having an eerie sense that the remembered winter chill had traveled through time to engulf them all.

As if by tacit agreement, no one mentioned the cause of the Havilland family's mourning. Felicity thought this omission extremely odd, as common courtesy would demand an expression of sympathy, albeit belated. When her father, Aunt Harriet, and Peter all began speaking at once, as if to warm the frigid gap of silence, her curiosity was honed even more sharply.

"Are you young pups here for—"

"You are looking well, Peter, I must—"

"Father, tell us about Emperor's—"

They all laughed uncomfortably. Strangely enough, it was Georgina, emerging from her reverie, who picked up the thread of conversation.

"Peter, did you chance upon Hubert while you were in London?" She spoke too casually, alerting Felicity to the fact that his answer was of vital interest to Georgina.

"No, indeed," Peter replied brightly. "That husband of yours is overly concerned with the financial matters of the realm these days, cousin. He judges his position to be most serious, scarcely poking his head out of the Exchequer, so

intent is he upon making his mark and ensuring your pride
in him.''

Georgina looked mildly disappointed in this revelation, and
Harriet chuckled.

"An ambitious young man, is my son-in-law. Mark my
words, Augustus, Hubert does not shirk his duty, as others
I might mention do.''

Augustus shot her a withering look. "By da . . . er, Jove,
madam, you do tax my patience. Will you bedevil me forever
over an incident that was not of my making?''

Harriet sniffed. "When Bellwood land is invaded by
scurrilous highwaymen, and when your own daughter is
nearly accosted—''

"What is this?'' Peter exclaimed. Under the rosy glow
provided by the port, he appeared distinctly pale.

Felicity had clung to the slimmest of hopes that the subject
would fade into history now that her brother had arrived.
She reconciled herself to another upbraiding and stiffened
her composure.

With perverse relish, Harriet recounted the tale, including
every small detail. When she had finished and sat back with
a grim complacence, Peter glared at his sister.

"Riding off after him was madness.''

Defensively Felicity stared back at him. "I own that I did
not pause to reason through the situation. It was an instinct
that I much regret at this point, having heard nothing but
how insane I was to have behaved as I did.''

When Peter's attitude did not bend, Felicity appealed to
him with her eyes. "Oh, do not be cross or think badly of
me, Peter. I was foolish, and simply outraged that such a
person would invade our property to rob Aunt Harriet of her
jewels.''

Even more than her reluctance to earn her father's disapproval, she could not bear to provoke Peter's wrath. All

her life she had looked up to the pedestal that he occupied in her mind, wishing only to be close enough to touch her golden brother. The prospect of his turning his back on her filled her with dread.

Still, he would not relent. "The branches are low through that stretch of wood. You might have been knocked off your mount. Sheba might have stumbled in the soft earth and thrown you. You might be lying dead at this very moment."

She lowered her gaze so that he would not read in her eyes how uncannily close he had come to the truth. "I am a decent horsewoman, Peter," she said softly. "You have often told me so."

Risking a glance at him, she saw his mask of anger slowly crack. Sighing, he grinned fondly at her. "Indeed, you are a superb rider. And all is well that ends well, I suppose. Still . . ."

"I vow," Felicity said hurriedly, "to think long and hard before I take such a risk again. You know that this was completely unlike me, Peter. I am usually the most cautious of persons."

"Again, I must agree with you, dear sister." Peter still smiled, but his grin looked forced and sheepish. "I am the risk-taker in this family, it appears."

Assuming he referred to his action in the wars, the action that had cost him the full use of his leg, Felicity smiled in sympathy at him. "I love you for your nature, dear brother. And I thank you for being concerned for my welfare. I promise that I shall take much better care in the future."

Much relieved, Felicity realized that throughout the exchange she had paid no heed to the reactions of the others gathered at table. With a quick survey, she saw that her father and her aunt seemed content that Peter had fortified their admonishings. But Justin Havilland's gaze startled her no end.

He stared at her as if he wished to pierce her soul with his dark eyes. He obviously could not believe that a well-bred young lady would ever commit such a wild, unthinking act as to dash off after a highwayman.

In a strange way that she did not understand, Felicity felt much satisfied that she had surprised him. And then her own thought startled her more than his gaze. Why should she wish to surprise this man? She was not certain that she even wished to have anything to do with him. He offered a pleasantly polite facade, yet she instinctively felt that he possessed a deeper, roiling core that both fascinated and frightened her.

After a few moments she turned away her glance. His intensity was foreign to her, since she came from a family who, excepting Felicity herself, spoke precisely what was on their minds when the ideas occurred to them, a family who wore their moods and opinions like brightly colored cloaks, easily identifiable to any who chose to look. Justin Havilland enveloped himself in a mist, occasionally allowing it to part and reveal the threat of a storm.

"Well, then," her father said, interrupting her reverie, "now that the subject is settled and we know that Felicity will keep her wits about her in the future, I am pleased to proceed to happier topics. Peter, my boy, are you aware that the race meeting is upcoming?"

Felicity was silently grateful to her father's near-obsession with his horses. He embarked upon a spirited discussion about his finest stallion's chances at the approaching race meeting. All joined in, even Georgina, who seemed to have been ejected from her preoccupation by hearing that Hubert labored away as usual. Felicity listened with relief until, as the roasted joint of lamb and minted peas were served, Havilland addressed her directly.

"And what is your opinion, Lady Felicity?"

Startled, she glanced across the table at him. Ordinarily,

when persons other than her father and Peter were present, Felicity kept her own counsel, having learned that discretion was by far the better course for her. She was so unlike the other young ladies to whom gentlemen were accustomed. But the challenge in Havilland's dark eyes would not brook a demure quiescence.

She inhaled deeply. "I believe that Khan, another of father's horses, has a better chance to win in that race," she said in a firm, clear voice.

Her father guffawed. "Better than Emperor? He is by far the finest in our stable."

Felicity, abashed at her bluntness, did not reply. But Havilland prodded her.

Again she felt compelled to answer, and she could not have said exactly why. Something in Havilland's demeanor simply required that answers be given to queries. "Emperor runs magnificently when he is the sole racer on the course. But when other horses are competing, he does not perform so well."

Raising a disbelieving eyebrow, Havilland murmured, "A grand racing horse who shies at the prospect of competition? I find that difficult to credit."

Felicity never had enjoyed being the focus of attention, much preferring the safer observer's role. She certainly was unused to the blatant power Havilland exuded, not to mention the effect it had upon her. Now, not only had he forced her out of that observer's protection, he seemed to be impugning her reasoning. She had long since learned to ignore hints and subtle prods. But he was issuing a challenge to her intelligence, and mayhap to her mettle.

Bristling, Felicity did not measure her words. "Like most males of all species, sir," she blurted, "Emperor is far more concerned with posturing and asserting his power. That, and his prowess at stud."

Aunt Harriet gasped and actually dropped her fork with a loud clatter upon her plate. Augustus and Peter wore stunned expressions, aghast that she had spoken before a relative stranger in such an unmaidenly manner of such an indelicate subject as breeding. Georgina merely looked perplexed at the fuss.

"I fail to understand—"

"Hush, Georgina," her mother muttered.

Felicity flushed with a mortified heat and wished mightily that she might suddenly awake to find this all a bizarre nightmare. How had she ever allowed this man to maneuver her into such a digraced position? Her *faux pas* loomed in reality, and even though the conversation eventually wended on through less volatile topics, Felicity could not bring herself to join in.

Yet, when she dared to look up, none other than Justin Havilland caught her glance. To her amazement, she noted a twinkle in his eye. The gentleman was amused!

His reaction so astounded Felicity that she neglected to lower her gaze, peering at him in perplexed astonishment. What manner of man was this, who appeared to be polite unto wariness, then powerfully inquisitive, but who fought to suppress a grin at her rude appraisal of the male species?

As if wishing to confess her further, Justin then relinquished a slight smile.

She would have preferred by far a disdainful smirk. Then she might have dismissed the viscount as a bully who entertained himself by causing the most flaming blushes in young ladies. But his smile was personal, almost intimate, as if only the two of them were present in the room. Indeed, no one else seemed to have noticed the exchange between them.

More disconcerted than ever, Felicity then concentrated upon her meal, even though she had to force even the smallest morsel past her lips. Counting each long minute until the dinner would end and she could retreat from the puzzle of who Justin Havilland was, she was overly relieved when the table was cleared. Aunt Harriet rose and announced that the ladies would take their coffee in the evening parlor while the gentlemen could enjoy their cigars and brandy. Felicity was on her feet immediately, knowing that she could take a polite leave of Justin Havilland and never suffer those demanding questions and that baffling smile again.

"Thank you, sir, for an interesting evening," she murmured, aware of the slight ironic tinge in her tone. "Mayhap you shall visit again when you are in the area."

Havilland rose courteously. Even across the table, she could feel his towering presence. A specter of his smile returned, but Felicity would not be intimidated. She kept her chin high.

"It has truly been my pleasure, Lady Felicity," he answered.

Try as she might, Felicity could detect no hint of wryness in his words. He sounded sincere.

Peter nearly knocked over his glass as he rose for the ladies to take their leave. "Perhaps you shall see him sooner than you think, dear sister. What do you say, Havilland? Will you stay with us for a while to choose a pair of horses?"

As he considered, Havilland peered intently at her, as if she would tip the balance in favor of or against his remaining at Bellwood House. Felicity bravely attempted to keep her expression neutral.

"If it is of no inconvenience to your family, Peter, I shall be delighted to stay."

"Good show, Havilland!" Peter said heartily, then leaned closer to Felicity. "Is that not a pleasant propa . . . er, proposition?"

Peter's slurred speech alarmed her, but not nearly as much as the thought of spending more time in the presence of the paradoxical Justin Havilland.

5

The following morning Felicity awakened and stretched languidly. Just as she began the enjoyable task of planning her day, she remembered: a guest was in the house, and one sure to disrupt her unique pleasures.

Sighing, she threw back the quilted silk coverlet and, padding barefoot to the window, drew back the heavy curtain. The lemony sun had risen not far above the horizon, but it promised a superb day. What a pity that she would be forced to waste it. For with Justin Havilland in the house, appearances must be kept. Ladylike pursuits would be all that she might follow. Her father would not welcome her into the stables as usual to discuss the relative merits of breeding a certain stallion to a certain mare. Indeed, he had nearly suffered an apoplexy on the previous evening when she had mentioned the word "stud."

As, indeed, nearly had she.

She still could not understand her own forthrightness. On the rare occasions when guests were present, Felicity was usually the soul of demure discretion. She had learned that if one were an interested listener, one need contribute only comments upon the speaker's conversation to be considered congenial. Nothing of one's own soul need be revealed.

And how fortunate for her that this be so! For on what topics could she discourse? Young women of her age deemed the bucolic country life she led a bore and rarely came to call. But when they did, she found discussions of needlework and the latest fashions far outside her realm of reality. A practical riding habit and a sturdy pair of boots were all the fashion that interested her. Gossip was mildly informative, but as most of the young women gossiped about eligible young men, Felicity again found herself stifling yawns.

With the gentlemen who came to visit, she was no more forthcoming. She could not embarrass her father by appearing too knowledgeable about topics of which women were supposed to know nothing. Thus she silently nodded and did not add to their discussions of oat fields and cattle and horses.

And so when confronted with the feminine spheres with which she was supposed to be familiar, she languished in boredom. And in those masculine arenas to which she might have added lively opinions, she was forced to leash her tongue.

Small wonder she preferred her solitude.

Sighing again, Felicity returned to her bed and rang for a chambermaid. In deference to Nanny's age, she had Milly help her with her morning rituals, so as not to rouse the older woman too early. On most mornings she would have Milly help her into a riding habit and spend the next hour or more in a brisk ride around the estate. But not today. Havilland and her brother would surely take advantage of the fine morning for a gallop of their own. And she had no desire to encounter Sir Justin at the stables. Heaven only knew what indiscretions he would elicit from her in that milieu.

" 'Mornin', milady," Milly chirped, entering the room. "And ain't it a lovely one."

She drew back the curtains at all four windows, while Felicity sulked in her bed.

"On such a fine day," Milly continued, oblivious of her mistress's mood, "yer pale green habit seems to be the jolly choice. Don't ye agree, milady?"

"No, I do not. Please bring me my breakfast."

Milly halted before the wardrobe and stared in surprise at Felicity. "Now, milady? Before yer jaunt about the grounds?"

"I am not riding this morning, Milly."

The maid hurried to her side, resting her hand upon Felicity's brow. "Is it ill ye are? Shall I fetch Nanny?"

"Certainly not," Felicity snapped, and pushed the girl's hand away rather more forcefully than she intended. For the third time in the space of a few minutes, she sighed.

"Please forgive me. I . . . I am simply tired. Rest is all I need."

Nodding dubiously, Milly departed for the kitchen.

Felicity had been awake not even half an hour, and even so, her vow to avoid Viscount Pentclair was grating on her. Last evening, after one sip of her coffee in the evening parlor, she had invented a head aching from exhaustion, and surprisingly, Aunt Harriet had agreed that they all had suffered a trying day. They had retired while Papa, Peter, and Havilland were still at their brandy and cigars, leaving the gentlemen to entertain themselves for the remainder of the evening.

So Felicity had achieved one reprieve, although upon reflection it occurred to her that the victory had come with uncommon ease. Aunt Harriet, ever the stickler for *comme il faut*, usually insisted on upholding the duties of a hostess, amusing the gentlemen with choice tidbits of gossip and games of whist, or pressing one of the other ladies present to play tunes upon the pianoforte. But Aunt Harriet apparently felt no such obligation toward Justin Havilland.

And now that Felicity thought further on the subject, Aunt Harriet had been far from her charming self with their guest. In fact, Felicity could recall no time at which the woman even had addressed Havilland directly. How curious . . .

Before she could ruminate further, Milly arrived with her breakfast. The maid set the tray across Felicity's lap and removed the silver domes, revealing eggs coddled to a turn, plump sausages, buttered muffins: all the elements of a hearty country breakfast.

But without her morning ride to pique her appetite, Felicity was satisfied after only a few bites. She asked Milly to remove the tray, and, after reassuring the maid a dozen times that she was not ill, she completed her toilette and chose a morning dress of yellow muslin sprigged with tiny green leaves. With her hair dressed and pinned, she dismissed the maid and set to amusing herself. Felicity intended to spend the entire day in her room, nursing a ''headache'' that would last a fortnight, if need be.

Her self-imposed exile lasted approximately two hours. She spent the time rather pleasurably at her writing table, penning entries in her journal. Such journals were a feminine family tradition, as Felicity had learned in her ongoing perusal of the various tomes in the vast library at Bellwood House. The Bellwood ladies' journals, lovingly bound in dark blue and gold, stretched back over the centuries, chronicling the events, both fascinating and mundane, in the lives of their illustrious family.

Her latest entries caused her much thought, for she needed to censor the amazing events of the previous day. The family honor demanded that she record only that a highwayman had robbed Aunt Harriet, not that Felicity had given foolish pursuit; that Peter and Sir Justin Havilland, Viscount Pentclair, had dined that evening, not that the gentleman had provoked such unladylike responses from her.

When she was satisfied with her writing, she put the journal aside and paced restlessly. Having spent little time in her room, having usually roamed the vast estate at will, and finding herself now bored to distraction, Felicity at last broke her vow.

Reasoning that the men would be occupied at the stables at least until the noon hour, she went downstairs to the library. Since her father's reading material ran mostly to journals of news in the county and stud books, which he kept conveniently close at hand in the smoking room, the library was Felicity's domain. A large room, stacked floor to ceiling with books collected over the centuries, it had been her haven, her font of knowledge and education. It still was.

She now spent some moments choosing a work in which to lose herself, to take her far away from Bellwood House and her problems of the moment. At last deciding upon a Latin version of Homer, she paused to fling open the tall, wide French window leading to the stone terrace, allowing the unseasonably warm breeze to scent the room with spring. Then she curled up in a big leather chair and began reading.

Felicity could not have said how much later she became aware of the voices. So immersed was she in her reading, she did not even hear them until they were almost directly outside the open window.

". . . made a fine choice with the bays, Havilland. That pair will present a fine picture, drawing your equipage. We've only to settle on a fair price."

"Er, I say, Father."

Even without seeing her brother, Felicity heard the nervousness in Peter's voice. Laying her book facedown and open on the arm of the chair, she quietly rose and went to stand at the corner of the window.

Peeking through the curtain, Felicity saw Augustus, Peter, and Havilland on the terrace. Her brother appeared more than nervous, his face pale and his brow furrowed as he nibbled at his thumbnail.

"Well, what is it, son? Are the horses not suitable, to your thinking? Speak up."

As Peter hesitated, Havilland stepped smoothly into the breach. "I am quite satisfied with the bays, Sir Augustus. And I accept whatever price you deem fair."

Papa chuckled. "Not much of a horse trader, are you, my man? One is supposed to dicker and bargain. Half the fun of it, don't you know."

"That is not the point," Peter blurted. "Justin is not the one to speak to about price. 'Tis I who must settle with you."

Augustus' look of puzzlement matched Felicity's own. Looking somewhat uneasy himself, Havilland merely frowned and stared fixedly at the stone terrace.

"Peter," he muttered so that Felicity had to strain to hear him, "this is unnecessary. I never—"

"No," Peter interrupted stoutly, his face suffused with misery. "Honor demands that the truth be told. I owe you a debt, and I fully intend to pay it off. I shall pay my father from my own funds, if the bays suffice to settle the debt."

"Certainly they suffice. But—"

"Then enough. Father, I shall pay."

Augustus turned scarlet, but controlled his anger. "How exactly was this debt accrued, Peter?"

"Gaming." With forced nonchalance Peter shrugged. "I was particularly unlucky at the faro table. Everyone goes through a bad run of luck occasionally."

"Indeed," Augustus muttered through clenched teeth. He drew a deep breath and turned to Havilland. "If you will excuse us, I have the details to discuss with my son. Come, Peter."

As he headed off back toward the stables, Peter shrugged and grinned at Havilland with a smile that did not reach his eyes. "Not to worry, my friend. The pater needs to blow smoke regularly. Good for his constitution. I shall return for luncheon, none the worse for the old boy's lambasting."

"Peter," Justin said in a tone more gentle than Felicity had thought possible of him, "I am not one to chide another for his gaming. I own to enjoying games of chance as well as the next fellow. But there is about your wagering an air of frenzy, of desperation, that is a bit excessive. Perhaps you should heed what your father will undoubtedly say regarding—"

"Spare me," Peter retorted harshly. "I am a grown man. Old enough to have lost the use of my leg in the service of the crown. Surely I deserve whatever pleasures that are left for me to enjoy. And if I choose to gamble away my entire inheritance, it is of no concern to you."

"You are quite correct," Justin conceded formally. "Please forgive my interference in private matters."

Peter grinned sheepishly. "Didn't intend to pop off at you like that, old man. I shall go down to the stables and allow the pater to vent his deserved anger on me. I shall even listen to every tenth word or so. Don't look so concerned. Father looks forward to my infrequent visits, that he might have cause to rail at me. 'Tis my filial duty to supply him with good reason. I shall see you at luncheon."

Setting off for the stables, Peter attempted a jaunty stride, but his limp ruined the effect. A wave of sadness washed over Felicity as she let the curtain drop and leaned warily against the wall.

She had known that her brother's fondness for the grape was getting out of hand. He could not hide the effects of too many three-bottle nights even on his occasional visits. But his excessive gaming was a new worry.

Lost in her thoughts, Felicity was startled to see movement in the room. Justin Havilland had entered through the French window, pacing around and running his fingers through his soft dark hair.

"That foolish boy," he muttered to himself.

He had not noticed Felicity and she froze against the wall. If only he would leave before he caught her so unabashedly eavesdropping!

Halting in his pace, Havilland began glancing around the bookshelves. "Where the deuce might Bellwood keep his brandy?"

Felicity realized that she was effectively trapped. Any moment now, Havilland's wandering gaze would come to rest on her. Sighing, she stepped away from the curtain.

"You will find the brandy on the third shelf, under the portrait," she said calmly.

6

Whirling around in the direction of the voice, Justin stared at Felicity in astonishment. She stood composed before the deep blue velvet window hanging, her hands clasped behind her back. The late-morning sun slanted across her, emphasizing the buttery yellow of her morning dress, burnishing her pale auburn hair with the patina of glowing copper. The smooth skin of her face reminded him of the texture of fresh cream, dusted with a faint blush of color across her aristocratic cheekbones. And yet, in the depths of her summer-sky eyes, he glimpsed a strength of purpose that belied her serene appearance. For a moment he remained totally still, almost entranced by the fetching picture she presented.

She took a step forward. "Shall I find the brandy for you?"

Quickly recovering himself, Justin shook his head. "No, thank you. I shall myself. Will you join me?"

As he expected, Felicity declined politely, but Justin sensed no surprise or disapproval that he should wish to imbibe at such an early hour of the day. She merely watched him with her clear gaze, and Justin felt vaguely uneasy, an unsettled intruder in her tranquil realm.

He located the spirits just where Felicity had indicated, on a glass-doored library shelf under the portrait, in a heavy cut-crystal decanter, along with four glasses. He poured a measure with a hand that surprised him with its slight tremor. Steadying himself, he brought the brandy to his lips, tilting his head back. Then he noticed the portrait more fully and realized that it was of the last Earl of Edgemont, the treacherous Octavius. Justin's eyes narrowed and his hand betrayed not even a hint of faltering as he drained the brandy.

Slowly Justin set the glass down and turned to Felicity. "Please forgive my intrusion. I was conversing with your father and brother on the terrace, and I had no idea that the room was occupied."

His words carried a subtle accusation of her eavesdropping, which gratified him. As he had learned long ago in the military, grasping the offensive position provided much more satisfying results than falling back on the defensive.

However, Felicity merely shrugged. "I gave no notice that it was occupied. Your mistake is understandable."

His eyebrows lifted. He hadn't expected her reply. Most women of his acquaintance would have demurred, perhaps even blushed mightily at having been caught out in their social *faux pas*, put immediately on the defensive. But this one had instantly reclaimed the offensive from him, without so much as the blink of an eye. Intrigued, Justin forcefully reminded himself that Lady Felicity was more clever than the vast majority of her sex.

He had sensed that quality in his first glimpse of her, more than one year's time ago, when he stood at the back of the family chapel at the last earl's memorial. Or rather, he nearly had been fooled by her apparently guileless expression, only to remind himself of the inherent actress present in all females. Once again he was struck with the notion of how dangerous she was, all the more perfidious for her air of innocence and openness.

He knew that he should retreat, withdraw to a position of

safety far from this house. And yet, she interested him. What manner of woman was she? What manner of Bellwood was she?

As he pondered, she moved gracefully to sit on the damask-covered settee. The sunlight framed her from behind, casting a faint golden glow about her hair and shoulders. Justin remained standing where he was, deciding to attempt to wrest the offensive position once more.

"The problem is overhearing what one is not meant to hear," he began steadily, "is that ignorance is often preferable to enlightenment."

"I disagree totally," she responded with equal steadiness. "I always prefer knowledge to ignorance."

"Indeed? Even if this knowledge is hurtful?"

"Especially so."

Without consciously intending to, Justin moved closer to her.

"Why 'especially so'?"

"When one knows the circumstances, one can deal with whatever the matter may be. Perhaps even help, in the case of a person for whom one has deep affection."

Her voice remained perfectly modulated, yet her eyes glowed with purpose. In them Justin read not an idle curiosity but a true concern for her brother's dilemma. Yet he debated with himself. In spite of her declaration, did she truly wish to know about Peter's problems? Before he could decide, she answered for him with an impatient wave of her graceful hand.

"I am not deft at the social dance of words, Viscount. Skirting the issue with delicate references seems a vexing waste of time to me. So please forgive my bluntness and allow me to ask you outright: How serious are my brother's gaming debts?"

Justin shrugged. "Not serious at all. As you undoubtedly

overheard, he had a run of bad luck at faro. A position in which any gaming gentleman has found himself from time to time. He was temporarily short of funds, and in truth, I found the prospect of his paying his obligation with a fine pair of horses more interesting, at any rate.''

She gazed firmly at him. ''It may surprise you to know that I am well acquainted with the terms of Peter's monetary settlements. My father, perhaps for lack of other family to discuss such topics with, is candid with me about family finances. And if Peter was 'temporarily short of funds,' it is indeed a serious matter. As Viscount Greenridge, he is entitled to the revenues from Greenridge lands, which amount to the substantial sum of—''

''Please!'' Justin raised his hand in alarm. ''It would be most unseemly for you to reveal that sum to me.''

Felicity bit delicately at her lip and cast her eyes downward. The fringe of her lashes shadowed against her nearly translucent skin. When she glanced up and spoke, her voice was quiet, but certainly not conciliatory.

''I confess that my bluntness at times steps over the bounds. But you must know that I am motivated by concern for Peter.''

Justin straightened. ''Then you will forgive me if I also speak bluntly. I am not certain that such a subject is fit for discussion with a man's sister. Even among gentlemen, it is a delicate matter to raise a question about the extent of a fellow's finances and gaming. Frankly, most of us consider such topics to be one's own concern. It's a matter of honor not to bring up such matters.''

''Oh, please do spare me the gentlemen's code of honor,'' Felicity said with a sigh. '' 'Tis perfectly acceptable to have vices, but one must never speak of them, especially in the presence of delicate ladies. Let me assure you that I am not inclined to the vapors. And let me further assure you that

I am not unacquainted with the vices of gentlemen. As I have told you, my father speaks quite freely with me.''

Justin could not repress a grin. ''The truth of that statement became abundantly clear after our discussion of horses at table last evening.''

Finally he had succeeded in rattling her. She blushed to the roots of her pale auburn hair.

''How gallant of you to remind me,'' she snapped, and Justin felt immediately contrite.

''My dear Lady Felicity. I seem to be begging your forgiveness in every other sentence I speak to you. This time, I truly ask for it. If the truth be told, I was delighted by your spirit last evening. Such candor is refreshing.''

As she gradually regained her composure, Justin was surprised to realize that he had meant every word. He had found her refreshing, but only when seduced by her air of openness. Yet, considering the family to which she belonged, such a belief was a difficult lump to swallow.

''If you set any store by my candor,'' she said softly now, ''please offer the same to me. Peter is . . . I have the most boundless affection for my brother, and I worry so about him. Do you think I have not witnessed with my own eyes the fact that he is drinking wine by the cask these days? This is not usual behavior. And now add to this his gaming . . . My brother is plagued by some personal demons. I must know the extent of his trouble in order to be of any help to him.''

Her eyes pleaded with Justin far more eloquently than her words. He nearly relented.

''I am not accustomed to speaking on such matters to ladies. However, I too have a deep affection for your brother. And I am not certain that your father's knowledge of the affair—''

''Rest assured,'' she said swiftly, ''that whatever you tell me will remain with me. I shall not speak to my father without your permission.''

Justin was startled by her quick perception, her knowing his thoughts even before he spoke them. She possessed a keen intellent that would not be diverted by his carefully worded speeches.

He moved to sit quietly opposite her on the settee. "Peter has seemed . . . excessive these days. We belong to the same London clubs, and therefore I see him quite frequently. I sense a peculiar fervor about him, as if he wishes to throw himself headlong into all that he does. As if sampling the wine, or the gaming, or the wom . . . er, well, as if moderation has no meaning for him. Almost as if he is obsessed with excess.''

"And from what does this obsession stem?''

Sighing deeply, Justin looked at her. She was watching him intently but evenly, appearing not a bit disturbed by his revelation. He glanced away, thinking.

"I believe his experiences in the wars may explain the cause of his obsession,'' he said softly, reflectively. "He is not the first lieutenant under my command whom I have seen with such urges. Being in battle changes their lives, and excess is the crux of warfare. All experience is heightened, the ultimate in intensity.

"They all come onto the battlefield fresh from their training, with their thirst for glory whetted by their shining ideals. They revel in the brightness of their uniforms and the smell of the new leather of their boots. They long to hear in the clash of swords the confirmation of their manhood. And instead, they hear the screams of the dying and smell the blood and the fear. And some of it is their own.''

Justin could see the scene now, as if it played before him on some vast mental stage. The faces once so cocky and confident contorted into masks of horror. The spotless uniforms as dirtied and bloodied as the ideals.

"When the first battle is over, they are dazed. Not so much by the grim reality of what they have witnessed as by a sense of near-betrayal. The reality was nowhere near what the textbooks had promised them. It was not a gentlemanly chess match where with clean hands one moved his pieces and out-witted his opponent. It was a fierce, filthy clawing, where one did not slay the enemy for some sense of winning a competition, but for the simple goal of survival. One slew the enemy merely to prevent him from slaying oneself."

"And Peter was no different from the rest."

Justin started and then blinked in alarm at Felicity. Whatever had possessed him! He had never voiced such thoughts even with men, much less before a lady. Men either knew because they had experienced the same, or they adhered to the code of honor that espoused bravery and glory, not reality. In either case, words were unnecessary. And women could neither understand nor withstand such brutal fact. How could he have let down his guard in such an unconscionable manner?

And yet, when he peered into her eyes, he saw compassion and comprehension, at least on the scale of which he had revealed the truth. Her look astonished him, but even more so did her words.

"I have ever suspected as much," she said quietly, with a slight wrinkling of her brow.

He could not help asking, "But how?"

"The accounts and pictures in books always have seemed staged to me. How could one place so many horses and swords so cleanly? It's only sensible that battles are not neat affairs, that there are blood and dirt and confusion. And when one adds human emotion to the picture . . . Men cannot be so different from women when they are a sword's length away from dying. Fear and pain must be more universal than that.''

Justin cleared his throat. "You must have spoken to Peter about this, to understand so well.''

"No,'' she said, surprising him. "I have tried to draw him out, but he refuses to speak on the matter at all.''

Puzzled, he continued to peer at her. "Then how did you know?''

She smiled with slight exasperation. "It's not that difficult. From what I've read of battles, from what I know about the physical properties of horses and people and blood, from what I have observed of human nature, it's a simple matter to imagine the reality.''

"You have a vast imagination,'' he commented briefly.

She shrugged. "I also read many books.''

"How many?''

Reluctantly, it seemed, she waved her hand in a sweeping gesture about the room. "Almost all of them,'' she admitted.

Now Justin was truly amazed. The library held a substantial number of tomes. Even if she exaggerated by half, she had ingested an impressive amount of knowledge. His mind raced with the implications of what she had revealed. Her intellect and obvious hunger for knowledge ranged far beyond any woman's of his acquaintance. Even beyond most men's.

His entire perception of her changed. The previous night at dinner, he had been struck again by her fragile beauty, and waited for her sidelong glances and dimpled smiles. After all, women of such obvious charms were prepared almost from birth to play the coquette, to snare a suitable husband. They plied their charms almost by rote when an eligible man was present. And from the near-frenzy Justin created when in London society among nubile young ladies, he knew he was considered prime material by marriage-minded mamas. But Felicity had surprised him. When she had not played the coquette, he had pegged her as a provincial maiden, content to while away her time peacefully in the country.

Now he condemned his judgment as foolishly naive. She was a Bellwood, and treachery ran solidly in her blood. With an intellect like hers, she was no simple country girl. Only a superb actress could project such an ingenuous air. A warning bell sounded ominously in his head.

And yet . . .

He must admit that she fascinated him. She was so unlike anyone else he had ever met, constantly astonishing him. Like a snake entrancing her prey, she drew his attention. The prudent move would be to climb upon his horse and gallop as far from Bellwood House as possible. But he found himself perversely wanting to remain, to uncover more of the mystery that was Felicity Bellwood.

"You are looking at me so strangely," she said now, shifting in her seat.

Recovering, Justin smiled. "I have never had such a strange conversation with a lady before."

"Am I discomfiting you?"

"Not in an unpleasant manner," he answered, surprised himself that he spoke the truth.

"Then would you please tell me more? I should like to know how Peter lost the use of his leg."

"He has never told you."

"No."

"Perhaps he would not appreciate my telling you now."

"Only because Peter, like most men, persists in the belief that women are the weaker sex," she answered dryly. "He fears that the story would offend my sensibilities to the point that I should never recover."

Justin felt a smile curving at his lips. "He does not know you well, does he?"

She returned his smile, revealing a small dimple in her

left cheek. "Unfortunately, no. I have no doubt that he loves me. But he prefers his preconceived notions about women in general. Perhaps they are less frightening than the truth."

"Or perhaps his notions are correct, and you are truly unique among women."

Felicity appeared slightly confused, as if she were not certain whether his comment was a compliment or a reproof. To his chagrin, Justin realized that his intent had been wholly complimentary. He also recognzied that his fascination with her had prompted such an uncensored reply. Once again he reminded himself to fortify his guard against her.

"The story, my dear viscount?"

"Oh, yes. Peter's injury."

For once, he did not need to organize his thoughts into an acceptable response. The memory of Peter's injury was firmly etched in his mind.

"A simple tale. During the third battle, the fighting was especially fierce. A French lancer came up on Peter's blind flank, and would have run him through. But at the last moment the Frenchman's horse stumbled in a small hole, and his aim was diverted. His lance struck Peter in the leg. I happened to be close by, and when I saw what had occurred, I pulled him off his mount onto mine and took him to the aid station. I had to return to the fighting, but I discovered later that the damage was rather extensive. Shattered his kneecap, or some such. Thus, Peter's limp."

Felicity glanced away with a hint of sadness. Finally she looked up at Justin, and he continued his story. "I have suspected that his urge to excess must be connected to his injury. As if he must make up for the things he cannot do now by doing what he can do in excess. He is especially distressed that his riding has been affected, I think."

She tilted her chin loyally. "He is still a good horseman. He is simply not superb anymore."

Justin nodded his understanding. Under normal circumstances, he might have left her explanation at that. But he felt compelled to shed further light.

"I have noted another paradox among men who have seen battle. Although they deplore the conditions they saw, they have some need to recreate the intensity. They cannot go for blood, but they can push their drinking and their gaming to the limits."

Gazing at him curiously, she asked, "Do you also feel such urges?"

His lips tightened. "I have had other troubles to occupy my wits."

What he did not add was that her family had been the primary source of those troubles. But the feelings of animosity did not rage in him as usual. He was preoccupied, gazing at Felicity. The sunlight still glowed about her, and yet he felt a sense of seeing her in a different light, an optical illusion he could not fully explain.

She seemed to wait for him to elaborate on his comment further. When he did not, she said simply, "Thank you. For telling me about my brother. And for rescuing him."

But Justin barely heard. He had realized the difference in his perception. He was seeing the awesome beauty in her strength. It seemed to give definition to her bones, to limn her face in a perfect glowing oval. No actress of even immense talent could put forth such a picture of real fortitude. At that moment, at least, Felicity Bellwood was real to her core.

The tall clock in the corner chimed respectfully. She stood, and Justin, recovering himself, did also.

"I must prepare for luncheon. But first I have a favor to ask of you."

Justin gave a slight bow. "At your service, Lady Felicity."

"Would you stay on here at Bellwood House for a time?"

Blinking, startled, Justin hesitated. "You wish me . . . Not to question your hospitality, but may I ask why?"

"If you stay on, so will Peter. I cannot help feeling that the ambience of London encourages his excesses. Perhaps here, in the slower pace of the country, he might find peace."

"I see your reasoning, but I fear I must respectfully decline. There are affairs to which I must attend . . ."

"Perhaps they might be put off for a while," she suggested gently, persuasively. "You have the perfect excuse to hand to Peter, you know."

Despite himself, Justin was intrigued. "And what might that be?"

"The race meeting in a fortnight," she said without hesitation. "Actually, it is quite the social event. If Peter could develop an interest in racing, he might transfer his obsession to a more healthy manner of expression. What do you think?"

Shrugging, Justin admitted, "That is a possibility."

Felicity stepped closer to him, her eyes shining eagerly. "And I am counting on you to give that possibility a sporting chance. You must, you know."

Justin raised an eyebrow. The only son of the Earl of Bennington was not accustomed to being told what he "must" do by anyone, much less a slip of a woman.

"I 'must'?"

Felicity smiled slightly. "Is it not the Chinese proverb that says when a man saves another's life, this man is responsible for the one he has saved? And has not this proverb been incorporated in the gentleman's code of honor?"

For a moment Justin stared at her. Then he laughed, a hearty booming laugh in which there was release and not a small measure of delight.

"My dear Lady Felicity. That you should live your life in the countryside and be so astute astonishes me. Whatever ladies' seminary did you attend that dispenses such an education as you have so obviously had?''

Her smile widened. ''This,'' she said, gesturing about the library, ''has been my sole seminary. And it has had the definite advantage, to my mind at any rate, of allowing me to choose the curriculum.''

Although Justin refrained from saying so, she had not learned her powers of persuasion from any book. They stemmed from the rare quirk of her innate intelligence.

''You have not answered my request,'' she reminded him. ''Will you stay?''

All his instincts told him to refuse in the most unambiguous terms. There was no predicting where his curiosity about and captivation with her would lead.

Yet with great amazement he heard himself saying, ''I should be delighted to avail myself of your hospitality. And I shall in all sincerity urge Peter to stay on too.''

Impulsively Felicity clasped his hand in hers. ''Oh, thank you so much, Viscount. I am truly in your debt, and I shall do my utmost to make your stay as pleasant as possible.''

Justin was at a loss for words, jolted by her touch. Her hand seemed to have a life of its own, soft and so pleasantly warm, alive and quivering with vitality. As if this vibrancy were contagious, it seemed to radiate into his own hand, shooting up his arm, lodging vividly in his heart. He caught his breath.

Did she feel the same pulsing tug, or did she merely react to his expression? She swiftly extracted her hand before he could tell.

''I must go now,'' she murmured, gathering her shawl. ''I shall leave it to you to persuade Peter to stay on.''

Justin cleared his throat, which had gone suddenly dry. ''It will be my pleasure.''

As she walked gracefully from the room, Justin stared after

her, his mind a battlefield with evenly matched opponents of dread and elation. No enemy he had ever faced had conquered him with such charm as Lady Felicity Bellwood.

7

Felicity leaned forward in concentrating as Sheba gracefully cleared the low fence in a striding leap. Grinning in satisfaction, she reined in the little mare next to Justin.

"Good show," he conceded, matching her grin.

His compliment pleased her more than she could own. Gazing at him now, so tall and straight in the saddle, his arms and shoulders taut under the black riding jacket, Felicity had to glance away, lest she reveal too much of her delight.

"The brook is just ahead," she said at last, pointing with her crop. "Shall we race?"

Before Justin could answer, Felicity nudged Sheba and went flying over the meadow. Behind her, she heard Justin's roar of protest at her quick start, and she laughed aloud. The countryside blurred past her in ribbons of tender green and delicate pink and yellow, the new leaves and budding wild-flowers a potpourri of spring scents.

Hearing the hooves of Justin's roan approaching, Felicity urged her mare onward toward a beech grove. The trail through the trees was too narrow to allow two horses abreast, so Justin was forced to fall in behind her. With the wind in her face and the loamy smell of the forest all around her, Felicity bent slightly, as she had seen the race jockeys do.

She arrived at the clearing first and halted Sheba with a triumphant hoot. Slightly short of breath, her cheeks flushed and her riding hat askew, she wheeled her horse toward him.

"I won!"

"You cheated."

"Oh, you protest because you are not as alert as you might be?"

"Hmph. The start of this race is not what I protest. I should be happy to give you five lengths' start and still win. No, I protest because you know this land, and you deliberately chose a narrow path on which I could not pass you up."

She laughed, and the sound tinkled through the clearing. "I own to my advantage. And I would be a fool to give it up."

"Keen-witted woman that you are," Justin commented dryly, but with a gracious deferral to her victory.

For a moment she sat upon her mount while Sheba contentedly chewed at the tender grass. In times past, Felicity would have blushed uncomfortably to be deemed a "keen-witted woman," for from most men the designation was not complimentary. But this man appeared to be different. He actually appreciated her wits, and indeed, seemed to encourage her use of them.

When she realized that she was staring at him, Felicity recovered herself.

"Peter should be along shortly," she said, gathering her composure. "I must admit that I was disappointed that he chose to come the long way round. He knows those fences are not beyond his ability to jump. Oh, well. I suppose I should be content that he agreed to come at all. Shall we unpack the picnic?"

"Capital idea."

Swinging off his horse, Justin tethered the roan loosely. Felicity walked Sheba to a nearby rock, intending to use it as a dismounting block. Just as her foot touched the stone, he was beside her, reaching out his strong arm. As she accepted his hand, his other arm went around her waist to steady her.

Suddenly Felicity's breath quickened, and she felt deliciously frozen in what felt like a partial embrace. His gaze captured hers, strengthening the illusion. As she stood on the rock, her face was at the same level with his, the velvety depths of her eyes and the firm planes of his face closer than they ever had been. A flash of dizziness swept over her, jolting her out of a near-trance, and she stepped down to the solid ground.

"I'll spread—"

"I'll just get—"

They both began speaking at once and broke off into self-conscious laughter. Then, as Justin fetched the packets from the leather bag slung across his roan, Felicity tethered Sheba and pulled down the heavy quilted blanket tied in front of the saddle horn. They spread out their picnic in a silence that Felicity fully appreciated. Still reeling from her reaction, she needed a few solitary moments to collect her thoughts. It seemed that she needed many such moments lately.

To evaluate the last few days as having been interesting, Felicity knew, was a distinct understatement. With the weather alternating between misty drizzles and outright downpours, they all had been confined to the house. At first, Felicity had considered the weather to be the worse luck, fearing that Justin and Peter would soon grow bored from the lack of activity. But Justin gratified her enormously, drawing Peter down to the stables and barns by day, getting into intense discussions with her father and brother about the relative merits of one horse to another, one crop of oats versus hay. All three of the gentlemen seemed to be enjoying themselves immensely.

With the ladies, the opposite appeared to be the case. Harriet received the news of Justin's and Peter's extended stay with tight lips and no comment other than that she preferred to be prepared in advance for houseguests. Felicity marked her reaction down to the fact that her aunt liked to think she was in charge at Bellwood House when she was in residence, and Felicity had offered the invitation. Still, Felicity pondered uncertainly.

Harriet, the most social of hostesses, had endured taking meals with the rest of them for the first few days. Then she gradually had withdrawn with one excuse after another: her rounds of visiting had exhausted her, or she had fallen far behind in her voluminous correspondence and must write letters to be sent across the empire. On the third day, she announced she was spending some time with Lady Ashford at Ashford Hall and departed rather abruptly.

Georgina meekly accompanied her mama, still wrapped in her preoccupation. Felicity was beginning to wonder about her cousin's relationship with her husband. Each post seemed to bring a long letter from one of Georgina's many friends, reporting on Hubert. Georgina discussed these reports freely with Felicity, but reacted to them inconsistently. Vacillating between fretting about Hubert's activities in London and indifference toward his behavior, Georgina only succeeded in creating confusion. Prudently, Felicity decided not to pry into her cousin's thoughts. At any rate, her own thoughts were stimulating enough.

She was enjoying herself tremendously and was astute enough to realize that the reason was obvious: she was being herself, and the day in the library was the bellwether of this novel behavior.

Once she had been caught in the act of eavesdropping, she had recognzied the fat as being in the fire and decided simply to let it sizzle. Her concern for Peter had overridden her reticence, and the results had astounded her. She was truly astonished that Justin had relented, had revealed a most sacred aspect of masculine life, the truth about men in battle. To Felicity it seemed the most precious of gifts, one offered in total disregard for her sex's sensibilities. For a few minutes Justin had opened a chink in masculine armor and revealed vulnerabilities; in turn, she had allowed him to witness her knowledge and intelligence. And when she realized this, she also noted that she had offered Justin a gift that until now she had bequeathed to no one, male or female.

What had prompted such largess, on either part? Felicity could not point to one word or one action as being the deciding factor. But after that day, her vexation and nervousness around Justin simply dissolved.

In the evenings after dinner, with Harriet and Georgina absent, and her father and brother engaged in endless double games of patience, Felicity and Justin naturally gravitated to each other. He began by inquiring as to which book she had been reading when he came upon her in the library. When she told him boldly that it was a Latin version of the *Iliad*, he appeared not so much dismayed as delighted. They had drifted into a lively argument regarding the various talents of Alcibiades and Agamemnon. That she should be discussing ancient Greek generals of lore and legend with anyone, that they both were stimulated far into the night, left Felicity both awed and exhilarated.

She felt so alive around him. And inevitably she found herself counting the days to the race meet with approaching dread. For now that she had glimpsed the excitement of speaking her mind, whatever would she do when he was gone?

She preferred not to contemplate such misgivings. Better, she reasoned, to enjoy things while she might.

When the dawn had broken in rosy tones, Felicity had been

elated. With her mental energies heightened and expended, she longed for the physical invigoration of a long ride. Peter and Justin had readily agreed to her suggestion of a picnic luncheon, and she set Cook to packing up assorted victuals with an eager flush to her cheeks.

Now she bent beside the crystalline brook to wash her hands in the icy water. The sun enveloped her in its warmth, and Felicity found herself smiling for no apparent reason. Justin was pouring one of her father's most valuable ports into earthenware mugs, and they both laughed at the incongruity, understanding and appreciating the irony without uttering a word. Those soundless exchanges that spoke volumes occurred more and more frequently between them lately.

As she unwrapped cold roasted chicken and relishes and sliced through the still-warm crusty bread, Felicity heard Peter approaching from beyond the brook. She waved to him with the loaf of bread and watched fondly as his horse splashed across the shallow water.

Peter's appearance certainly had improved. A healthy glow banished the gray pallor of his skin. And although a vague hauntedness still flashed in his eyes now and again, the dark half-circles beneath them had disappeared.

After he had swung down stiffly from his horse, Peter enthusiastically accepted the napery she offered him, in which she had wrapped generous cuts of bread spread with sweet butter and large portions of chicken. Her heart warmed to the evidence of his reawakened appetite. Only when he quaffed the wine Justin handed him in one long swallow did her pleasure falter.

But once again, she reminded herself to be grateful for the changes Peter's week in the country had wrought in him. To her thinking, any improvement was welcome.

"Ah, this place brings back fond memories," he said,

stretching out on the blanket and resting on one elbow. "When I was a lad, on warm summer days I liked to wade in that brook. Caught a few fine trout, too."

"Yes," Felicity added, "and you insisted upon chasing me away when I wished to engage in your fun. Rude lad that you were."

She smiled to show him she meant no reproach.

"What, and bear Nanny's wailing when I returned you wet and bedraggled, when I would be expected to protect you from the elements? Not on your life." Peter shrugged. "Ah, begin at the dawn of childhood. In truth, you far preferred playing with your dolls."

Felicity lowered her gaze, but not before she caught Justin's glance. She could tell that he knew that Peter had no notion of how far from the truth his perception was. But neither moved to correct her brother.

"Speaking of old days," Peter continued, "I saw Henning as I was leaving the stables."

"Oh, dear," Felicity laughed. "Please do not tell me that he was still complaining about our riding over his pastures when we were children." She turned to Justin. "Sir Edmund would become frightfully upset. He actually claimed we made his cows' milk sour from startling them!"

Peter chuckled. "No, the old boy has mellowed in his old age. His wife must have been quite the harridan, because her death has had the most amazingly positive effect on him. Suddenly he has become quite jovial. He's even entering a horse in the race . . . meeting . . ."

Peter's voice trailed off, and he glanced almost guiltily at Justin. Puzzled, Felicity looked from one to the other of them, searching for some clue as to why Peter had so abruptly clamped his jaw, as if he wished to swallow the words he had just spoken.

Justin's face remained implacable, giving no hint as to what Peter regretted saying.

"Do you expect that Sir Edmund's horse has a chance of winning?" Felicity asked, still uncertain of Peter's guilty glance. "Better than Papa's?"

"Oh, no," Peter said, much relieved, it seemed to Felicity. "Why, no one in the county has even the slimmest of chances against Bellwood stock. As I was saying to Father this morning . . ."

Her brother went on to boast with pride about Emperor, and the conversation turned to the upcoming race meeting. It did not occur to Felicity until much later that neither Peter nor Justin was bothered in the least by this topic.

Reinforcing her determination to push away any worry that threatened her current happiness, Felicity dismissed the entire incident from her mind. She let the spring air and sunshine lull her into contentment.

8

Augustus gazed in openmouthed astonishment at the sight of his sister-in-law lifting her skirts with obvious distaste and stepping gingerly through the stable.

"What the deuce are you doing here?"

"A question I am asking myself at this very moment," Harriet muttered. "But since Mohammed refuses to come to the mountain . . . Augustus, really. Is there not at the least a neutral ground upon which we might meet? This place is too disgusting to abide."

Replacing on a rack the bridle he had been lovingly mending, Augustus wiped his hands on his ancient riding breeches, frowning. "I have a tremendous amount of work to do, madam," he protested stoutly. "If the servants aren't up to snuff, find someone to train them. Or give them the sack and hire new. I have no time to listen to your silly household complaints. They are none of my concern."

Harriet sniffed. "This complaint should concern you, Augustus. It is regarding your daughter."

As she had anticipated, the mention of Felicity pricked up his ears. "What about Lissie? Hasn't gone hell-bent for leather after another highpad, has she?"

"Certainly not. And please mind your tongue. I am in no mood to endure your profanity."

"Well, what, then? By dam . . . er, drat, madam, you do try my patience."

Harriet gave him a long-suffering grimace. "The feeling, my dear Augustus, is entirely mutual. But I refuse to speak to you in the midst of all this . . . effluvium."

"Eff . . ." Augustus' expression wrinkled in total perplexity. "What the . . . Whatever are you . . ." At last comprehending, he released a loud guffaw. "You mean the horsesh—"

Harriet's hand snapped up in an unmistakable command to halt immediately. Closing her eyes, she scarcely breathed her words. "Do not even contemplate it."

"My deepest apologies," Augustus mumbled, barely controlling his devilish grin. "Perhaps you would care to step outside."

Harriet pressed her kerchief to her nose and sighed in deep relief. "Please."

Some yards upwind of the stables stood a stately oak tree, which had grown on the spot for nearly two hundred years. Augustus led Harriet there now, and gallantly spread his dusty coat on the wrought-iron bench encircling the trunk. Harriet peered at the coat resignedly.

"Oh, well. My dress was ruined the moment I left the house." She sat.

That she suffered such abominations even grudgingly should have set off bells of alarm in Augustus' head, she thought. But the man was a bit addled by all the time he spent with those infernal horses of his. Apparently he could not fathom that only the most dire of circumstances would have brought her this far from the house.

"By the way," she said abruptly, "where is Felicity?"

"Er, I believe she took a picnic luncheon down by the brook."

"A picnic! Augustus, where are your wits?"

"What is wrong with a picnic? Food tastes just as good from one's hand as from a fancy plate."

"Oh, Augustus," Harriet groaned. "Such talk from an Earl of Edgemont! And typically, you miss the point entirely."

Pacing back and forth before her, Augustus gestured impatiently. "So what is this problem concerning Felicity?"

With studied importance, Harriet settled herself on the bench. "I have pondered this for a long time. Indeed, I felt compelled to abandon Lady Ashford to rush back here to tell you this. 'Tis far and away long past time that Felicity was wedded."

Augustus blinked at her for a moment; then his features drew into a stormy frown. "Out of the question," he blustered. "Felicity is a mere child."

"Oh, really?" Harriet smirked. "How old is she, Augustus?"

He, who could rattle off the dates upon which each of his many horses had first seen the light of day, mumbled, "Why, she's seventeen, or eighteen—"

"She'll be twenty in six weeks' time," Harriet interrupted smugly. "A poor excuse for a father you are, completely unaware of that fact."

"I know my own daughter's age, madam. I merely was counting up and hadn't got there yet."

"Hmph. At any rate, it's a scandalous turn of events. Here she is, the only daughter of the ninth Earl of Edgemont, embarking upon her third decade in an unmarried state. Scandalous, I tell you."

"Numbers are not the only indication of one's readiness for marriage," Augustus protested. "She's just a girl—"

"Have you looked upon her, truly looked upon her lately?" Harriet demanded, exasperated. "She is a woman grown. I must own that my own problems kept me from noticing until the first night I returned here. Did you not note her appearance at dinner? As luck would have it, when she discards those shabby riding habits for a proper gown, she is particularly beautiful. At the least you can be grateful for that attribute. As the situation stands, it may be uncommonly difficult to make the brilliant match her station requires."

"Difficult! By . . . er, Jupiter, madam, any man worth his salt would be on his knees begging to be leg-shackled by my daughter! That is, if she were of an opinion to wed."

Brushing his comment away, Harriet said practically, "What has her opinion to do with anything? Of course she wants to be wedded. All ladies do. It is the function of our sex, to wed the appropriate man and produce the appropriate heirs. Family honor absolutely decrees it."

"That is not Lissie's concern," he insisted. "Peter will wed eventually and secure the family honor."

With a smile one used for a thick-headed child, Harriet replied sweetly, "And what would happen should every parent of a daughter think as you do? Who, pray tell, would there be for Peter to marry?"

When Augustus had no answer, Harriet continued. "Believe me, Augustus. Whether Felicity has said so or not, she is aching to be wedded. It is the nature of the species. Well she knows, or should, that the alliance of great houses is as much the duty of the woman as the man. She merely has had no experience in the hunt. So we shall aid her in her apparently unspoken quest. In order to make a good match, we simply must tailor the search for a husband to Felicity's peculiar circumstances."

"What peculiar circumstances?" Augustus rubbed his jaw in frustration. "Madam, you do insist upon speaking in the damnedest riddles."

Harriet flashed him a warning look until he shrugged an

irritated apology for his profanity. Satisfied, she attempted to explain.

"When planning a campaign of such importance, one must gaze with cold detachment upon the various virtues and flaws of the woman. In simplest terms, which I must remind myself to employ when speaking to you, one must accentuate the virtues and disguise the flaws."

Augustus' expression was downcast. "You speak of my little girl as if she were a piece of goods to barter."

"In a manner of speaking," Harriet responded calmly, "she is. Detachment, I tell you. It is absolutely essential. If one allows emotion to cloud the issue, one merely becomes confused and perhaps misses the one brilliant match that opportunity provides. Now. Do you agree that it is time your daughter be wedded?"

"Well . . ."

"If naught else," Harriet persuaded, "think of what may happen to her once you are gone. Do you wish to die not knowing what will become of your daughter? Or do you wish to be secure in the knowledge that the proper husband will care for her long after you are buried?"

Defeated, Augustus sat down beside his determined sister-in-law. "What shall I do?"

Patting his knee in encouragement, Harriet smiled. "Fortunately for you, I am well-versed in these matters. Look what an advantageous match I made for Georgina."

"Yes. The girl is so delighted with her husband, she spends half her time roaming about the countryside with her mama, while Hubert saves the financial empire in London."

Slowly turning her head, Harriet stared at him icily. "Georgina," she said in measured tones, "is ecstatically happy in her match with Hubert. As a good daughter, she merely wishes to keep her widowed mama company for a time. You find something questionable in that?"

Shrugging noncommittally, Augustus was sharp-witted enough to refrain from answering.

"Now, if you are done with your snide comments, are you prepared to listen to me?"

"Have I a choice?"

"Not if you wish to see your daughter well-married."

"Very well. What must I do?"

Harriet enumerated on her fingers. "First, we must choose the appropriate gentlemen to whom she will be introduced. This will provide a guest list for her come-out. On the advantageous side, she is the daughter of an earl, with, I presume, sufficient properties settled on her for her dowry. Therefore, we may choose from the cream of society in preparing this list. On the side of disadvantage, however, are her age and her isolation from the *haut ton* up to this point. People will wonder what is wrong with her that her come-out has been delayed overlong. In the balance, I believe that curiosity, if naught else, will weigh in our favor. Whoever we invite will gladly accept."

Her brow wrinkling in concentration, Harriet spoke as if Augustus were not even present. She was wrapped in a dilemma over which she had confident control. So different from her last dilemmas, which defied her considerable ability to manifest her will, it was therefore a problem she relished.

"Now for a more pressing quandary. The usual manner of presenting a girl on the Marriage Mart is to set up head-quarters in London. *Tout le beau monde* is within easy reach, and after the come-out ball, a suitable girl is showered with invitations to crushes and routs and musicales. But Felicity has spent her entire life wasting away in the country."

She shot Augustus a withering glance, accusing him mutely of causing the unfortunate situation.

"And even in the country, where social events are of the most informal tone, the girl is lacking in the requisite graces.

So I fear that in London, where she will undoubtedly feel out of her element, she will not feature herself to her best advantage. That is the flaw we must disguise. The solution to this puzzle has been vexing me all week.

"However, and I must own this is a difficult potion to swallow, the answer came to me just a while ago. 'If Mohammed will not come to the mountain . . .' Remember my saying that to you? Well, it occurs to me that this is the perfect resolution. If we will not come to London, London will come to us."

"I fail to understand—"

"Certainly you do. You are the male of the species, and have no clue as to the vast talents of persuasion an accomplished lady possesses. You are not expected to know these things. Else, how would those talents work?"

Befuddled by her "feminine" logic, Augustus merely looked ahead.

If Harriet noticed, she ignored him. "Now, I shan't bore you with the other details, so allow me simply to list the essence of Felicity's virtues and flaws. Just so you will see what we are up against. Her virtues are that she is a comely girl and that she is your daughter. A perfect form and absolutely impeccable bloodlines. Those are terms which you should understand well enough. And you should thank the heavens for them, because her flaws are serious."

"For the life of me," Augustus said softly, "I fail to see even one."

Harriet shook her finger reprovingly at him. "Remember the essential detachment. You are looking with a father's eyes upon her. Allow me to particularize these flaws: Her priorities are sadly out of balance. She prefers riding to paying calls, the stables to the drawing room. However, I believe this is not an inherent flaw. She simply has had no experience in the proper milieu. In addition, her housekeeping skills are woefully lacking. The servants actually are fond of her!''

''Is that so terrible?''

''Well, certainly! The proper attitude for servants is one of respect, not affection. One loses all authority elsewhere, and soon the second footman is missing a button and there are spots on the glassware. Totally unacceptable. No man would stand for it.''

If Augustus thought to declare that he, by definition most certainly a man, never gave the slightest attention to the second footman's buttons, he wisely remained silent.

''Her wardrobe is a disgrace,'' Harriet continued relentlessly. ''Her day dresses are fraying at the cuffs, and I would not permit even my maid to wear the drab little affairs she calls dinner gowns.''

Augustus sighed. ''Well, Harriet, you seem to have this dilemma all mapped out. For what purpose do you need me?''

''To open the purse strings,'' Harriet replied bluntly. ''I will not dither you about, Augustus. A vast sum of monies will be required. Triple the number of seamstresses for her wardrobe. A swift and total refurbishing of accommodations for dozens of guests. Food and drink for the lot.''

Glumly Augustus regarded his sister-in-law. ''The funds are no problem. But what chance has my Lissie of securing a proper husband?''

''Oh, a fine one, I think,'' Harriet declared, perversely cheerful now. ''All those flaws of hers can be disguised or corrected with a bit of effort.''

Her mood changed just as abruptly to ponderous. ''But the one flaw that is the most serious, and the one that will be decidedly difficult to conceal, is the slant of her mind.''

''What are you blathering about? Lissie has a fine mind.''

''And that is all the trouble, my dear Augustus. Most girls

are encouraged to set their wits to their true purpose in life: pleasing a man who will eventually offer for her. And then keeping him pleased by providing a tranquil, amusing, and edifying household for him. So her education consists of learning to perfect her needlework, and to play gracefully at the pianoforte, and to encourage the witty conversation that so delights the gentlemen. Felicity's education has been wholly inadequate.''

With a slight inclination of her head, Harriet gave a concession.

"I fear I must accept part of the blame for that. I was occupied bringing up Georgina, and I failed to supervise Felicity's governess as I should have. I fear that so long as the girl did not bother her, the governess left Felicity much to her own devices. And then, when Georgina attended Miss Baxter's, I should have insisted upon Felicity's attendance there too. But instead, I was taken in by your reasoning that with her melancholy regarding Peter, off to the wars, she would thrive far better in her own environs. I bowed to your decision to allow her to remain at home.''

Augustus' dubious expression said plainly that he had some difficulty in swallowing her definition of her own "blame," but Harriet once more ignored him.

"And that is where your culpability lies, Augustus. You allowed her to educate herself, to fill her head with whatever she chose, giving her free run of the library. As a result, Felicity . . .'' Harriet closed her eyes and spoke the words reluctantly. ''. . . .has trained herself to think like a man.''

"You make such generalized assumptions, Harriet. And if the girl uses the wits God gave her, what difference does it make in the manner of her thinking?''

"What difference! Why, all the difference in the world, Augustus. One's actions are directly tied to one's thoughts. How can she act as a woman should, while thinking like a man? 'Tis an impossible situation, Augustus, and if you cannot see it, you had better open your eyes. What will be her reply when her husband comments, for instance, about the state of the Foreign Department? Will she say, 'Such a pity, dear,' and leave it at that? Or will she argue with him throughout dinner about the merits of one policy for dealing with France versus another?''

Harriet looked aghast at the very idea. "What gentleman would abide such impertinent behavior from his wife? None of my acquaintance, I assure you.''

"Oh, I don't know about that,'' Augustus said stubbornly. "She and Havilland spend half the evening arguing over dead Greeks and military strategy. He seems to abide it quite swimmingly.''

Harriet gasped and jumped to her feet, startling them both. Clasping her bosom dramatically, she moaned. "Augustus Bellwood, you have driven a nail straight through my heart. *How* could you mention that cad's name in the same sentence with Felicity? Have you no decency, man?''

A bit guiltily, Augustus chewed at his lip. Yet he apparently felt compelled to defend Havilland. "He's not a bad sort. Actually quite knowledgeable about horses. And he's done a world of good for Peter, staying here in the country.''

Harriet stared down at him coldly. "Have you forgotten already? Are you so heartless and disloyal that you choose to ignore the fact that the Havilland family is directly responsible for your brother Octavius' death?''

"Justin had nothing to do—''

"Oh, didn't he?'' Harriet asked scathingly. "Should he not have had an iron-fisted control over the situation? Was there not a certain person in his family whom he failed to stop before my husband was destroyed? Sit there and tell me that, and I shall call you a bald liar and never think twice of it.''

Raising a placating hand, Augustus said mildly, "Now, Harriet—"

"Do not even contemplate an attempt to pacify me. I am in the right, and if you were truly a gentleman worthy of the Bellwood name, you would call him out to avenge the family honor, not offer him the hospitality of your home."

Finally Augustus had reached the far side of enough. "And it *is* my home, madam," he barked in no uncertain terms. "I shall have whom I choose here, and tolerate no reproofs from you. In truth, vengeance tastes poorly to me and, in my opinion, would only serve to alert the public to what we have managed to keep a secret so far. To my mind, the family honor requires—demands—no further action that might cause the tragic details surrounding Octavius' death to come to light now."

Harriet pressed her lips together, but made no response. Her own education had taught her that at certain boiling points, a woman should recognize the prudent course and defer.

"How long will that man be here?" she asked quietly.

"I've no idea. Months, for all I care."

"And I cannot be two places at one time," she murmured in distraction. "I cannot manage all the arrangements for Felicity's come-out from here. I must go to London, at least for a time."

Suddenly she plucked at her brother-in-law's arm pleadingly. "Augustus, I beg you. If you value Felicity's happiness and well-being, please, please watch the situation closely in my absence. Do not allow Havilland to weave any sort of spell about her."

"I credit little chance to that," Augustus said, patting her hand awkwardly. "But if it is of such importance to you, I shall be mindful of the situation. Here, here, old girl. Buck up now. You will manage a brilliant match for my daughter, and we all shall live happily ever after."

Smiling weakly, Harriet nodded.

"Er, one last item, Harriet," Augustus said, hesitating. "I believe that the announcement to Felicity of a husband-hunt should come from you. She'll be more amenable, the news coming from a woman, I think."

"For once, my dear man, we are in total accord." She straightened, regaining her aplomb. "I shall inform Felicity when the time is right. You will allow me that discretion?"

"Of course, of course," Augustus agreed hastily. "And I shall place an account at your disposal. Do not consider the slightest thrift, Harriet. I want the best for my girl."

With a slight smile, Harriet considered that Augustus might live to regret his generosity. But he would never regret the absolutely perfect match she intended to make for her niece.

Harriet permitted her brother-in-law to escort her back to the house. An endless list of things to do began forming in her mind; Harriet could scarcely wait to get started.

And could scarcely afford any delay. The sooner Felicity was removed from the scurrilous influence of Sir Justin Havilland, the better for the entire Bellwood family.

9

The afternoon breeze, unseasonably warm for early April, wafted gently around Justin. The soft rustling of new leaves, the muted gurgling of the brook, and the melodious chirp of nesting birds combined in a peaceful melange that quieted the spirit. Indeed, Peter had been so lulled that he had fallen into a deep sleep. At least, that was the reason to which Justin preferred to attribute his friend's nap. He did not like to think that the half-bottle of port Peter had drunk had anything to do with his lethargy.

Justin himself relaxed on the blanket, resting on his forearms, his booted feet crossed. So many troubles had roiled his mind in the past few years, he had quite forgotten the restorative value of the countryside. And quite missed it, too.

Glancing to his right, he smiled as he gazed at Felicity. She had drifted off, picking wildflowers, humming to herself slightly out of tune. Removing her riding bonnet, she used it to hold fistfuls of blossoms. Wisps of her auburn hair fluttered in the breeze, catching sunbeams in flashes of golden red.

A tender wave of a nearly forgotten emotion swept through Justin, catching him by surprise. Perhaps the serenity of the glen had woven a spell about him. Or perhaps, more ominously, the Bellwoods had. For whatever reason, Justin realized with some trepidation that the emotion, tentative but clear, was affection.

Such a feeling seemed so alien to him that he wondered if he ever had felt so before. For whom did one usually feel fondness? Mentally he ran through a list of his family. For his father, he had the greatest respect, but fondness was not a part of their tie. His mother had died when he was too young to recognize her presence; so if an attachment was there, he did not recall it. His three sisters were so many years older than he, with penchants for marrying foreigners. They all lived out of England now, and had since he was a schoolboy. With some guilt, Justin realized that he had not even thought of them in years.

Surely in the beginning, in his first months or weeks with Alice, he had experienced affection. But to his chagrin, when he tried vainly to pull some instance, some long-buried memory of tenderness from his mind, he drew only blank spaces.

Was it possible that he, a grown man of eight-and-twenty, had never felt any affection before?

The vary notion left him feeling indescribably bereft.

So which emotions could he ascribe to himself? As a major in the military, his attitude toward his troops had been one of pride, loyalty, and respect. As Viscount Pentclair, his sense of duty, honor, and ambition ruled his life. With Alice, at least at the start of their marriage . . .

He seldom thought about those days, much in the way he would ignore a wound rather than dig at it and produce more pain. But now he gave a probative poke to his memory, and then caught his breath when the first hurtful images flashed in his mind. The colors of his past with Alice were intense, even violent. Passion, greed, and jealousy, now glazed over with a deep coating of bitterness. And shame.

Agitated, he mentally bound the wound and concentrated on ignoring it. He had no desire to destroy the sense of calm and restoration that the wooded glen provided.

But the tranquillity allowed the feelings of affection to roll back over him. Hesitantly, and with great caution, he prodded at them. With a start that jolted him to his bones, he realized that the feelings were, indeed, all connected to the Bellwoods.

He never had enjoyed himself so much as he had in the past week. Sir Augustus projected a contagious enthusiasm for his horses, and Justin had caught it willingly. The easy camaraderie among men, the good-natured competition, the smells of saddle soap and leather and the earthy scent of the horses themselves, all brought back the happier portions of his military life.

Peter elicited his compassion, for in truth, Justin saw in the lad a reflection uncomfortably close to resembling himself. And indeed, he felt a sense of responsibility for Peter, as if in saving his hide, Justin had undertaken an obligation to see that Peter's life was not spent in vain pursuits.

His reactions to both men were ones that Justin could understand, if not fully accept. What truly confused him was his response to Felicity.

He had glimpsed her intelligence and mental vitality in the library. But on that very night, while deep into a lively discussion about ancient Greeks, he suddenly had felt a tingling sensation, like the not unpleasant prickling of the skin just before lightning strikes. It had taken him hours to fall asleep when at last he reluctantly retired. His mind raced through points they should have made and reveled in the ones they had. He never had felt so alive before.

Felicity delighted him in ways both complex and simple. He was moved to the same smile by her brilliant analysis of Agamemnon and the sound of her cheerful, off-key humming. Even more, he sensed between them a silent bond, so that often, few or no words were necessary. Their thoughts seemed to transfer from one mind to the other without benefit of verbalization.

What in the world was happening?

Could it be, was it possible, that he was developing a *tendre* for her? The idea appeared totally preposterous, considering who she was.

For the thousandth time, Justin reminded himself that she was, above all, a Bellwood. His sworn enemy. How could he feel affection for one from whose family he had vowed to exact vengeance?

The puzzle left his mind whirling, and Justin leaned back, closing his eyes. He always had prided himself on his vast powers of concentration. Now he trained those considerable powers to the task of focusing on the singing birds, the splashing brook. Peace was restored.

Feeling a movement beside him, he blinked and shaded his eyes from the sun with his hand. Felicity knelt close, spilling the flowers she had collected onto the blanket. He rolled to his side, his elbow crooked, resting his head upon his hand.

"Oh, forgive me," she said. "Did I wake you?"

"I was not sleeping," he assured her. "Just listening to the lullaby."

Felicity smiled. "Why is it that I am certain you are referring to the birds, and not to my singing?"

"You sing charmingly," he protested.

"Only if one has no ear for harmony."

They both laughed softly.

"Peter looks like a little boy," she noted, "so relaxed and peaceful. Perhaps his demons are abandoning him after all, chased away by the songbirds."

"Perhaps. I hope so."

"Have I expressed my gratitude to you for keeping him here?"

"Only one hundred times," he answered dryly.

"Then allow this to be number one hundred and one. I am so delighted that you are here."

They both glanced at each other and then away. Justin found himself wondering if her delight stemmed solely from her concern for Peter, or if he himself played any part in her enjoyment. To his amazement, he realized that he fervently hoped that she also found pleasure in him.

At a loss for words, he simply looked on as Felicity began weaving the wildflowers into a chain. He could not recall the names of the blossoms, if indeed he ever had known. She noticed him watching her and smiled.

"Daisies and bluebells, and are these pink ones columbine? I'm not quite certain. This is surely watercress. It will add a peppery scent to the chain, and if we are still hungry, it will provide a lovely snack."

Justin laughed aloud at the thought of munching away on her wildflower chain. Her fingers worked deftly and gracefully, the motion faintly hypnotic and decidedly captivating.

When she was done, she fastened the ends of the chain together. Then, leaning toward him, she placed the circlet on his head.

"There," she said playfully. "I crown you King of the Glen, monarch of all your survey."

As she drew back her hand, Justin caught it and, without thinking, pulled it to his cheek.

"Including you?"

Felicity blinked at him in confusion. For a moment he held her hand, feeling the delicate warmth against his cheek, catching the scent of watercress on her fingers. Her eyes were more velvety than the softest of bluebells, her hair the essence of fiery sunlight.

Finally she gently withdrew her hand.

Justin stifled a groan. Whatever had prossessed him?

Attempting to rescue the moment, Felicity spoke with a flash of her former playfulness. "I cannot be your subject, King of the Glen," she said with a tremorous smile. "I am *in* the glen, 'tis true, but not a part of it."

Oh, how wrong you are, Justin thought urgently. She was sunlight and wildflowers and murmuring birds and cascading brook. She was life and spirit, and serenity too. He wondered how in the name of heaven his soul had existed for so many years without knowing her.

Justin swallowed hard, and wished longingly that the bottle of port were not lying empty on its side. He stood up, and the wildflower circlet fell to the blanket.

"Here, here," Felicity said. "You must take more care with the crown jewels."

She was trying with all her might to jest casually. But Justin heard the quickening in her pulse, the confusion that matched his own.

"I stand reproved." He bowed, grinning, and scooped up the circlet, looping it around his wrist. "I shall deposit it immediately into the treasure chest."

With a look akin to relief, Felicity began packing up the remains of their luncheon. "We must be getting back. Father will wonder if we have gone to the next county."

Silently, almost by rote, Justin began helping her. His mind was scarcely aware of his actions.

These feelings for Felicity, this attraction and fascination and tenderness, could not be permitted. They all were illusion, at any rate. They must be. And he was a man exceedingly vulnerable to illusions.

Alice was a perfect case in point. He had been attracted to her too, only on a darker scale. From the very start, his desire for her had been veined with a deep thread of forboding, which he, in his besotted state, had regrettably ignored. Alice, too, had been a woman of keen intellect, and of sharp enough wits to disguise her treachery with a deceptive exterior. Felicity Bellwood was no doubt cut from the same cloth.

This entire day must have been an illusion, brought on by the deceptive lulling of the glen. With her deftness, Felicity had woven a trance about him, a far more insidious weaving than her trick with the flowers. He was in imminent danger of falling under her spell. A Bellwood spell.

Only one course of action remained for him. He had promised to stay for the race meeting, and he would never contemplate going back on his word. So he was bound to stay at Bellwood House for another week. But the moment that the last horse crossed the finish line, he would be gone. He only prayed that he could concentrate on finding the reality of Felicity's duplicity. His resistance to her charm was weakening. Without erecting a solid guard against her, he might well find himself completely powerless.

At that moment Peter stirred and sat up, rubbing his eyes.

"I must have popped off," he said, blinking as he came more fully awake. "What did I miss?"

Felicity grinned. "Not much. Only the coronation."

She and Justin both laughed at Peter's perplexity. When the satchel was repacked and the blanket rolled up, they climbed on their horses. This time, Peter aided his sister to mount from the rock.

"Shall we go back the long route, with Peter?" Felicity asked nonchalantly.

"Yes, indeed," Justin hastily agreed. "I should like to see that part of the land."

She directed her mare across the shallow brook, with Peter following her. Justin trailed behind.

In the middle of the brook, he shook his wrist and the crown of woven flowers fell free. Justin watched intently as the circlet bobbed in the water and began floating slowly away from him downstream.

10

Felicity placed a velvet marker between the pages and closed her journal. Or, more precisely, her secret journal. She still kept the official version, in the same blue-and-gold binding as the previous journals of the Bellwood women, faithfully documenting in it the mundane chronicle of her days: occurrences on the estate, the daily weather, all the ordinary details of her outer life. But a few days ago she had felt that she would burst if she could not make a record of her real self, her manifesting inner life. Thus she had begun her secret journal, describing her thoughts and feelings in a book bound in discreet dove-gray leather. Only by penning an account of the changes in her life could she hope to understand them. And such astounding changes they were. For the first time in her life, she was alive and real.

What liberation it was to speak and act just as she thought! No longer must she weigh every word before verbalizing her thoughts, judging the effect upon the one who would hear her. Quite a task it had been, that constant weighing; as a result, she largely had remained silent much of the time. Now she owned to becoming quite the chatterbox, allowing her words to spill out the moment a thought occurred to her. As a bonus, she had discovered, to her secret delight, that she was capable of a delicious wit. With her ability to elicit laughter from those around her, Felicity's life was a much less somber affair than usual.

Her father and Peter had seemed to accept the changes in her casually, if a bit distractedly. They smiled more often in her presence. But the one who seemed to appreciate her free expression, to willingly abet it, was Justin.

He represented both the cause and the effect of her freedom. He provided the impetus for her boldness in speaking her mind, and he seemed to relish the revelation of her true self. With this encouragement and acceptance of her, it seemed he stood right beside her, tearing down the wall brick by crumbling brick.

One aspect of the tumbled walls that she had not expected was the simultaneous liberation of her emotions. Over the years, she had become inured to feelings, bricked up as they were along with her real, inner self. Now emotions freely swirled over the boundaries from inner suppression to outer comprehension, startling her with their intensity. She experienced her feelings sharply and clearly now; happiness seemed a brilliant warmth, and sadness a throbbing ache. Yet she probed her feelings tentatively and was reticent to express them freely. Only recently was she becoming accustomed to disclosing her true thoughts; she was not yet prepared to reveal her feelings too.

And perhaps the most surprising effect of all was the heightening of her senses. Suddenly she was highly sensitive to sights and sounds and touches. Yesterday, in the glen by the brook, she had felt nearly intoxicated by the enfolding sunshine, the clean spring scent of the trees. And by the touch of her fingers against Justin's skin.

Her hand still tingled from the warmth of his cheek. She could smell the sunlight in his dark hair, see the depths of the forest in his dusky eyes, feel the sweet softness of his breath upon her face. The experience had left her dazzled, and slightly confused. Strange, how her awareness of her sharpened senses and of Justin were liked intrinsically together.

Last evening had been less lively than the previous nights, and Felicity had been privately grateful for the relative silence. Change was manifesting in her so swiftly, she needed periods of silence to absorb everything. She and Justin had played chess, and concentrating on their moves had made the need for conversation slight. Justin too had been in a quieter mode, although he played with an almost fierce competitiveness, as if victory signaled more than merely winning at a parlor game. The evening had ended early, but Felicity had not minded. She could scarcely wait to get to her writing.

She hugged her secret journal to her bosom now and smiled reflectively. Then a light tapping at her door roused her from her reverie.

"Enter," she called, sliding her secret journal under the pillow of her chaise longue.

Milly stuck her head inside the room. "The seamstress from the village has arrived, milady."

"Splendid! Bring her up."

On an impulse out of character for her, Felicity had summoned Mrs. Watkins nearly a week ago, telling herself that with a guest in residence, family honor decreed that she look presentable. She had chosen fabrics and styles of her preference, ordering five day dresses and the same number of dinner gowns to be made up, along with matching slippers and undergarments. At last the seamstress was delivering her order.

"Good morning, milady," the seamstress said cheerily, her cheeks still reddened from her climb of the stairs.

"Good morning, Mrs. Watkins. Come in, come in."

With Milly's aid, the seamstress brought in armfuls of

carefully tied packages. One by one she unwrapped the parcels, revealing a rainbow of fashions.

"Oh, Mrs. Watkins, you have done an excellent job, and in so little time. These gowns are lovely."

" 'Twas my pleasure, milady. I was right pleased to stitch up something other than a riding habit for ye."

Felicity laughed. "In former days, a riding habit was all I required to be well-dressed. Now other interests place me in need of a decent wardrobe."

Milly ran a roughened hand over the garments. "Oh, milady. Why not put one on now?"

"Why, Milly, I think I shall. Which one shall I choose?"

"The pink one, milady. That's me favorite."

"Then the pink one it will be."

As the maid helped her out of her shabby gray dress and into the new one, Felicity smiled. How Aunt Harriet would protest her wearing this shade, considering the hue of her hair. But the color complimented her, the pink having golden tones, reminding Felicity of fresh peaches. Insets of creamy lace, embroidered with tiny blue flowers, filled the neckline and cuffed the sleeves. Blue silk over kid slippers completed the effect.

"Oh, milady," Milly cried ecstatically, clasping her hands together. "Won't ye make a pretty picture at luncheon!"

Felicity turned to Mrs. Watkins. "It fits perfectly. Thank you so much."

"Anytime, milady."

"Actually, I hope you mean that. I should like to order another ensemble, for the race meeting next week. I realize I am giving you unforgivably short notice again . . ."

Mrs. Watkins, who was seldom, if ever, entrusted with the wardrobes of nobility, waved away Felicity's apologetic tone.

"It won't be a problem, milady. My assistants are good

girls, and they would welcome the work. What did ye have in mind?''

For a few minutes they discussed fabrics and styles and trimmings, finally coming to an agreement.

"I'll have the . . . er, ensemble ready for you in six days' time," Mrs. Watkins promised. "With a fitting day after tomorrow. Will that suit you, milady?''

"Yes, certainly. And again, I thank you for accommodating me on such short notice.''

"And wouldn't I be delighted to stich up anything for you at any time, milady. Even a new riding habit.''

"Well, I shall keep that in mind," Felicity said, laughing. Then she turned to the maid. "Milly, show Mrs. Watkins downstairs. Dobbs will settle the account with her. Then you can return, if you will, to see to these gowns.''

"Aye, milady.''

After they had left, Felicity spent some moments before the pier glass, holding each gown up and humming to herself. No more practical grays and dark blues for her. She would drape herself in the colors of spring flowers and sunshine. Her outer self would match her inner self.

When Milly returned, she announced, "Lady Harriet wishes to speak to ye, milady. She rang downstairs and asked that ye come to her rooms.''

Felicity suppressed a groan. Until now she had avoided her aunt successfully. When Harriet had returned unexpectedly from Ashford Hall the day before, Felicity had seen her only in passing. Her aunt complained of a tired headache, and had taken dinner on a tray in her rooms. Privately, Felicity had been relieved. Aunt Harriet would surely not approve of the new Felicity. But since she also was forever railing at her niece about the disgraceful state of her wardrobe, perhaps the fashionable gown would distract her.

Impulsively Felicity slipped on a pair of blue enameled

ear bobs and dabbed rosewater at her throat. Then she practiced a demure smile in the pier glass until she was satisfied with the results. Inhaling deeply, she set off down the hallway.

When she had knocked and been acknowledged, Felicity entered her aunt's room. Harriet was sitting at her writing table, scribbling furiously, surrounded by a jumble of papers. She glanced up at her niece and set down her quill.

"Good day, Felicity. And how are you faring?"

"Quite well, aunt. Although I am a bit disappointed by the rain. Yesterday's sunshine was so glorious!"

"Yes, indeed. Well, come, come. Take a seat by the fire."

Felicity did as she was told, sitting quietly on the settee before the hearth.

"I have something of great importance to discuss with you."

Oh, no, Felicity thought bleakly. Harriet had obviously discovered another missing button on a footman, or dark spots on the silver. She braced herself for another lecture about her negligible ability at supervising the servants.

"You are wearing a new gown," Harriet said suddenly.

"Why, yes, I—"

"A comely style, but women with coppery hair should never wear pink."

Felicity bit her tongue.

Peering at her niece intently, as if measuring her by some silent standard, Harriet finally nodded. She came to sit next to Felicity and stirred the fire.

"There is no chill like that of an ancient country house," Harriet mused aloud. "Even the London town house produces more warmth."

Felicity gazed at her aunt curiously. Apparently the discussion she had in mind did not include lectures. But why was her aunt dissembling? Harriet was never one for hesitation or idle chatter. Poking at the embers, she seemed to be gathering her thoughts before speaking. At last she replaced the poker and turned to her niece with a suspiciously bright smile.

"Well. It appears that the anniversary of your birth is approaching in a few weeks."

"Yes. The fourteenth of May."

"And a milestone, of sorts. You will be embarking upon your twentieth year."

Actually, thought Felicity, the twenty-first, if one considered the year before the first birthday to be the year one. However, she prudently did not point out the discrepancy to her aunt.

"In light of this date, your father and I have made some decisions regarding your future."

Felicity blinked in alarm. "What decisions might those be, aunt?" she asked cautiously.

Harriet sighed. "Well, I am not one for talking around a subject Felicity, dear, I have some wonderful news. Your father has decided, and I heartily concur, that it is time to find a husband for you."

"What!" Felicity jumped up and stared at her aunt. "That cannot be true."

"Certainly, it is true," Harriet said mildly. "It should have been done two years ago, at the least. I declare, Felicity, I thought you would be pleased."

Pleased! Felicity was filled with an abhorrence near to panic. She did not want to marry, to be subservient to some man and agree with whatever silly opinions he voiced. She had no desire to be responsible for a household, forever vigilant against untidy servants and tarnished silver. Yet she sensed that if she rebelled openly, Harriet merely would more stubbornly insist. Swallowing the lump of fear in her throat, she tried to smile.

"I . . . you caught me off-guard, aunt. I simply had not expected . . ."

"But of course you did, my dear. At your age, Georgina had been wedded more than a year. Most Bellwood women have produced a first child, even a second, by this time. Surely you expected to do the same."

Feeling suddenly faint, Felicity sat back down. "Aunt Harriet, I . . . do not know how to respond."

Patting her hand cheerily, Harriet said, "You are overwhelmed with excitement. I fully understand. This is the most wonderful time of a girl's life, preparing for her come-out into society."

"Come-out?" Felicity managed to ask weakly.

"Yes, indeed. One must initiate a search for a husband by introducing the eligible girl to the *haut ton*. Do not fret, my dear. We shall feature you to your best advantage. Scores of eager young men, those of the highest water, will flock to court you. It will be the grandest lark."

To Felicity it sounded more the grimmest punishment. So stunned was she by the announcement, her wits seemed to have flitted away. She searched her mind for some rebuttal that would halt Harriet in her tracks. But, infuriatingly, her thoughts scattered.

"Now, I realize," Harriet went on, seemingly unaware of Felicity's discomfort, "that you are woefully lacking in the social graces. Never fear, I have a plan to combat that defect in your upbringing. We shall hold your come-out ball right here at Bellwood House! Is that not the most charming idea? It will draw much attention to you, a ball in the country in the stead of London. Fortunately for you, your auntie has many, many friends in *le beau monde* who will accept what is not done, in her case. They will be curious to see if I can accomplish such a feat in the hinterlands. And you, my dear, will be more comfortable in your own surroundings, and therefore more relaxed and sprightly. Nothing repulses a man so much as a fretful, overwrought girl.''

Oh, mercy, Felicity thought in dejection. According to her aunt, not only must she face such a trial, but she must be laughing and gay while enduring it.

"When is all this to come to pass?" Felicity asked quietly.

With a long-suffering sigh Harriet replied, "Well, at the optimum, I should like to hold the ball before you reach twenty. But unfortunately, that gives me too little time to prepare. So, late June, I expect. The workmen will require at least that long to refurbish Bellwood House.''

"Workmen?" Felicity asked weakly. "Invading the house and tearing it apart?''

"Refurbishing, dear. We must prepare for dozens and dozens of guests. I've written to Lady Ashford, and I am certain that she will agree to open Ashford Hall to the overflow. And if needs be, Lady Butterfield will be only too willing to accommodate twenty or thirty also.''

Harriet squeezed Felicity's hand and smiled slyly. "Are you not indeed fortunate that your auntie has sown the seed of so many favors, and may reap a harvest of favors in return, for your sake?''

Crestfallen, Felicity turned her head to hide what was sure to be a devastated expression. The thought of strangers first traipsing through Bellwood House to redecorate, then another bunch living there for God only knew how long, dismayed her mightily. And then, as reward for abiding such invasions, she would receive a husband under whose thumb she might remain for the rest of her days.

"Felicity, dear, pay attention. Now, I shall be truthful with you. There are some obstacles, I must own, considering your situation. But with my talents and your father's generosity, we shall accomplish the near-impossible. We shall find the perfect mate for you.''

Inhaling deeply, Felicity slowly turned to her aunt. "I cannot credit," she began slowly, "that my father has agreed to all this."

"Agreed? Why, certainly he agreed. In point of fact, he told me to spare no expense in creating the perfect come-out for you."

"I cannot accept that he wishes to send me away." Her tone was edged with hurt.

"Felicity. Do you wish to be a burden to your father? He is not a young man, and he is the earl. Do you not suppose that he imagined a far different life for you than the one you currently lead? And do you not suppose that it causes him great pain to think he might never have grandchildren—*your* children—to dandle upon his knee? And leaving all that aside, mark my words: eventually the shame of a spinster daughter will be the death of him."

Was Papa truly ashamed of her? Felicity had never considered so before. But perhaps his feelings were walled up in the same manner hers had always been. Her mind reeled with confusion, and she trusted none of her perceptions. Suddenly she felt compelled to speak to him, to learn the truth.

She jumped up. "Aunt Harriet, I just now remembered that . . . that Papa asked me to be certain to come to the stables before luncheon. Something urgent, regarding the race meeting or some such—"

"Dear me, Felicity," Harriet interrupted with ill-concealed impatience. "Here I am making all these complicated arrangements, and you wish to run off. We have not even discussed bringing the modiste down from London, or the decor of the ball. and I should very much like to see the state of your dancing skills. Many a girl who has tripped up in the ballroom has found herself tripping up with an eligible bachelor, you know."

"Well, we have some time for that, aunt," Felicity said, already edging toward escape. "I leave all the details in your capable hands."

Beaming smugly, Harriet replied, "A wise decision, my dear, and one you will not regret. Very well, Felicity, you may go. But please do change your dress first. I see that the rain has stopped, but that vile stable will ruin your gown at any rate. Although I must own that I fail to see the tragedy in that prospect. Coppery-haired girls should never wear pink."

Felicity scarcely heard her. She ran out of the room and down the hall, pausing at her room only to pull on a pair of heavy boots and to snatch up a hodded cloak. Then she sped downstairs and toward the stables.

11

"*Papa!*" Felicity called urgently as she rounded the corner into the stable. "Papa, where are you?"

She heard his voice faintly from the tack room. "In here, daughter."

She found him soaping a saddle. The gleaming leather and the clean, polished scent filled Felicity with the most curious sense of loss.

Noting and misreading her expression, Augustus said defensively, "Not one of the grooms can do this job half as well as I. And if you must know, I enjoy it. Gives me time to think."

She shook her head. "Fine, Papa. I have no quarrel with your soaping. I rather enjoy the scent myself."

Pleased, Augustus wiped his hands on a much-used rag. "What are you doing down here? You are not dressed for riding."

"Papa, I must speak to you. It is vital."

After peering at her for a moment, Augustus sighed and spread a blanket over a bale of hay. He gestured for her to sit, but Felicity was too agitated to be still.

For a moment he watched her pacing in the small confines of the tack room. Finally he sighed resignedly. "You have been speaking to your aunt."

Felicity stopped and stared at him in supplication. "Oh, Papa, tell me it is not true. Tell me you do not wish to send me away."

"Send you away? Certainly not. Er, what exactly did Harriet tell you?"

"That I am to be wedded. To some man! Oh, Papa, can you credit such an idea?"

"Well, certainly I can. Look here, Lissie. You are a woman grown now. It is far past time we settled your future."

"But, Papa," she pleaded, "my future is settled. I shall remain here caring for you, making a pleasant household for you. I know that my housekeeping skills are dreadful. But I shall improve, I vow that I shall. I'll put my head together with Dobbs and we will produce the most well-run household in England. I can do it if I set my wits to it, Papa. Just watch."

Augustus brushed aside her promises impatiently. "Well you know how little I care about well-run households. So long as my meals are on time and I have a clean shirt to wear, I am content. No, Lissie, the household is not the point. Look at you, my girl. You are far and away ready to wed. I only blame myself for not noticing sooner."

"Oh, Papa, I have absolutely no desire to marry! Do my wishes not count even in the slightest?"

Clearing his throat brusquely, Augustus declared, "Naturally you wish to marry. All girls do. 'Tis simply that you have not considered the idea fully. Think on it, and you will see that I am correct. Imagine your happiness with a strong wellborn husband, and a quiverful of children in the nursery. Does the idea not warm your heart? See, I knew that it would."

Felicity sighed helplessly. "I like children well enough, Papa. The problem with them is that one must marry in order to produce them."

Augustus' eyebrows shot upward. "By damn, Lissie, I should certainly hope so."

"But do you not see? I do not agree that marriage is worth the price. I will not do it, Papa. I refuse to marry, and my decision is final!"

"Felicity, stop all this nonsense immediately!" Augustus raged. "You know that you want to be wedded, and that is the end of the matter. You shall be."

Felicity hung her head, a huge wave of sadness sweeping through her anger. Apparently her father had accepted her new, integrated self only so long as she was smiling and witty and making him laugh. But he would not acknowledge her true self, her honest feelings, when this manifestation of her conflicted with his preconceived notions of the goals to which young ladies should aspire.

"Have I no voice in the matter at all?" she asked quietly, plaintively.

Augustus' answer was blunt. "No. Because apparently you do not know your own mind. That is why God gave you a father. So that I may think practically when you refuse to do so. So that while you dawdle, I may make the decision that will secure your future."

Her glance reflected her sense of betrayal. "I have never known you to be so cruel."

"And I have never known you to be so willful and stubborn!"

Drawing her cloak about her, Felicity set her jaw and looked at Augustus straightforwardly.

"Then, my dear Papa, you have never known me at all."

She whirled and ran from the stables before he could witness the tears filling her eyes.

Felicity slammed the heavy library doors with all her might.

"Silly, stupid man!" she said of the father she had near-adored all her life.

"Present company excepted, I should hope."

Gasping, Felicity turned quickly with a swirl of her cloak.
The voice emanated from the leather chair next to the fire,
the one she always chose in which to curl up and read, and
belonged to Justin Havilland.

"What are you doing here?" she snapped without thinking.

"Reading the most interesting chronicles," he replied
mildly, "written by an ancestor of yours. Eleanor, wife of
the fourth earl. She had quite a pithy wit, this Eleanor. I hope
I have not overstepped the bounds of hospitality by helping
myself to your books."

"No, no, certainly not," Felicity said a bit more calmly,
discarding her cloak in distraction. "She is quite witty."

"I suspect it is a family trait. Along with a remarkable
talent for losing one's temper."

Her eyes flashing, Felicity came to warm her hands at the
fire. "Well, the events of this morning warrant a fit of
temper! This is merely the most disastrous day of my life."

"Justin made no reply, watching her. In accordance with
her dramatic statement, she appeared more agitated than ever
he had seen her. Anger and frustration crowded into her
expression, and her soft, pliant mouth was drawn in an un-
compromising line.

"Has the empire collapsed?" he asked lightly, attempting
to lighten her dark mood.

Felicity sniffed. "Hmph. Well and good for you to jest.
It's my life that has just been condemned to imprisonment."

She appeared so indignant, her brows drawn together, her
pale cheeks flushed the same warm shade as that of her dress.
A lovely feminine dress, he noted, and one that suited her
far better than the usual drab colors she wore. But the hem
was wet and dirtied, and on her feet she sported, incon-
gruously, a pair of mud-splashed riding boots. He smiled.

"You find my anguish amusing?" she asked sharply.

"No, no," he hastened to assure her. "I merely wonder

at your vehemence. Surely things are not as dire as you suggest.''

Felicity stared at him scathingly. ''You *would* make a comment like that.''

''I would? Why, pray tell?''

''Because you are a man!''

Defeated by her logic, Justin simply looked at her. The hood of her cloak had mussed her hair, so that long auburn strands of it curled about her shoulders. With Felicity in such a state, looking so forlorn and bedraggled, his resolve to steer a wide path around her melted a bit.

He rose. ''Here, sit down a moment.''

''I do not wish to sit down. And I am perfectly capable of knowing when I wish to sit and when I wish to stand!''

''I am certain that you are. Well, then, would you care for a brandy?''

She blinked at him. ''Before luncheon?''

''For medicinal purposes only. You appear chilled to the bone.''

''Well . . . Perhaps you are right. I am shivering, but I vow it is because I am so angry I could scream.''

Justin went to the cabinet and poured her a splash. Reconsidering, he poured himself another. When he returned to the fireplace and handed her a glass, he saw her peering pointedly at him.

He shrugged. ''One should never drink alone. It is a rule.''

She made no comment, but took a rather larger sip than was prudent. Justin winced as she gasped and coughed.

''Feeling better?''

Pausing to catch her breath, Felicity finally nodded. ''Yes. I vow that I am.''

Apparently she wished to sit now, for she dropped wearily into the leather chair. Justin pulled up another seat, decided that he, too, wished to sit, and did.

"Now. Tell me about the disaster."

"I do not care to speak of it," she said stiffly.

"Very well."

They sat in silence for all of ten seconds.

"I cannot believe what they intend for me!" Felicity blurted.

"Who is 'they'?"

"Aunt Harriet and my father. My own father!"

"What is it that they intend for you?"

She set her glass down on the butler's table and fixed him with an incredulous stare. "They intend to marry me off!"

Strangely, Justin felt his heart skip and heard his mind shout: No. Then he chided himself for such a ridiculous reaction. Of course they intended for her to marry. She was of age, and well-bred, and undeniably beautiful as well. She made a valuable pawn in any dynastic match they wished to finesse. And the Bellwoods' matrimonial ambitions were none of his concern, at any rate.

So why did the prospect of Felicity's marrying strike such a chord of disharmony in him?

Shaking off his thoughts, Justin cleared his throat solemnly. "Marriage is a serious matter. But not necessarily a disaster."

He hoped that his expression did not belie his words.

"Yes, a disaster," she insisted. "What you, being a man, fail to understand is how debilitating, how confining marriage is for a woman."

"Oh?"

"Yes, indeed. Can you imagine me forced to simper and blush and agree with every ridiculous statement that a man utters? I surely shall expire from the exertion."

"Surely."

"And then there are the horses. Do you suppose he will permit me to putter about the stables the day long should

I choose to do so? Absolutely not. And instead of daily rides, I shall be forced into an eternal round of visiting other simpering, blushing ladies, talking endlessly about how cheeky the servants have become.''

"Perish the thought," Justin murmured.

"And," she continued like a wound clock destined to tick away, "he will almost certainly expect me to entertain his boring cronies, and embroider his vests, and fetch him his evening brandy. Not that he ever would offer *me* a glass."

In her distraught condition, Felicity nonetheless retained her charm. Never had a woman spoke so candidly with him, and in truth, she scored telling points. He had never paused to consider that a woman might feel as leg-shackled in a marriage as a man might. Still, he could not witness her misery without attempting to pour a small draft of balm on her dismay.

"You paint such a grim picture. But surely all men are not cut from the same cloth. You merely must choose a man who will allow you your freedom."

"That man does not exist!" she answered vehemently. "Even those men whom I believed might do so will not. My father, even Peter . . . men are all the same. If I do not fit the mold that they have cast for me, then they never so much as dream of tossing away the mold. They assume I must change to fit it. My preferences are not granted even the slightest consideration."

She jumped up and began pacing.

"Would your preferences include another brandy?" Justin asked, hoping to calm her once more. "Unlike that mythical tyrant of a husband of which you spoke, I should be delighted to offer you one."

Suddenly she halted in mid-step, her back to him. Slowly she turned and peered at him, sizing him as if she had never seen him before.

"Yes," she said slowly and reflectively. "You *did* offer me brandy. And you allowed me to rant, and never once told me that I was speaking nonsense."

Felicity took a step closer to him, a strange glow in her eyes. "And you allowed me to spill out my feelings, and did not deny my right to them. You *are* different."

A curious unease settled over Justin. He watched in fascinated trepidation as Felicity's expression gradually changed. Her mouth curved in a slow smile, and the glow in her eyes ligthened.

"Of course!" she declared, delighted with relief. "That is the solution. I shall marry *you*!"

Justin gasped, and the empty brandy glass slipped from his hand and rolled harmlessly across the Aubusson carpet. "What!"

Felicity rushed to him and knelt by his side. "Do you not see?" she asked earnestly. "It's a perfect solution! You allow me to be who I truly am. You do not care a fig if I am opinionated or if I speak my true thoughts. And I should not mind if you chose to stay out all the night gaming, or drinking, or whatever it is that men do when they stay out all the night. You would be totally free to pursue your desires, and I would also. It would be such fun!"

Justin stared at her, aghast. She had no notion of what she was saying. But beyond that, she would never know what an eerie, chilling echo her words were to ones he had heard years ago. Alice had offered him essentially the same business deal: total freedom on behalf of both parties, with the convenience of a marriage to protect their reputations.

Totally enamored of Alice, bewitched by her seductive charms, and obsessed by a powerful desire for her, he had agreed. And the results had been the near-destruction of his family honor. And of him.

With a trembling hand Justin rubbed at his brow. He should

have listened to his instincts. Felicity was no different from Alice, and posed the same dangerous trap for him.

"Well?" she asked brightly now. "What do you think? Is it not a capital idea?"

With great effort Justin pulled a veil over his churning emotions. He forced a wavering smile.

"It is not possible," he murmured.

"Why not? I believe Papa would be delighted. He gets on well enough with you."

"Felicity . . ." Justin hesitated. Even after at last recognizing her duplicitous nature, he could not be cruel. "I have been married—"

"Oh!"

Felicity moved back on her heels and stared at him, her blue eyes rounded.

"I had not thought that you might already have a wife," she said in a small voice.

"Well," he said reluctantly, "strictly speaking, I do not. She died a little more than a year ago."

"Oh," she said once more, and Justin could see evidence of her mind working reflected in her gaze. "The first night you came to dinner. Papa asked about grouse hunting with your father, and you said your family had been in mourning. It was for your wife, was it not?"

Pressing his lips together, Justin finally conceded, "Yes, it was."

She appeared stricken. "Oh, but how awful for you, and how cruel of me! I beg your forgiveness. I had no idea . . ."

Justin shifted in his seat, feeling distinctly uncomfortable with her sympathy. "Her death occurred more than a year ago," he said tightly. "I am recovered."

He could not erase the slight tone of irony from his voice, but Felicity appeared not to have noticed. She seemed at an unusual loss for words.

"At any rate," he found himself saying, "I am not good husband material. I fear you shall be forced to look elsewhere for your savior."

"Yes," she agreed meekly, "I suppose I shall."

Quietly she rose and seated herself in the leather chair, unaware of how poignantly her hands drooped over the sides.

"It will not be a simple matter," she murmured, shaking her head.

"No. Most likely not."

Laughing slightly, she rolled her eyes. "You have no notion of how excited Aunt Harriet is. Can you credit that she actually is planning to refurbish Bellwood House? She is holding my come-out ball here, in June. Even now she speaks of teams of workmen, and seamstresses from London, and no doubt some dandy of a dancing master to perfect my waltzing skills."

Tears gathered in her eyes. She looked at Justin and said simply, "I cannot bear the thought of so many strangers poking about my life."

Despite his substantial misgivings regarding her, despite his instinctual fear, Justin felt his heart melting. She looked so fragile and forlorn in the big leather chair. Her tears glistened unshed, her eyes resembling deep blue pools.

"You can survive," he said gently. "You are a woman of exceptionally strong character. Perhaps you may even enjoy some of the fuss."

She smiled at him through her tears. "Do you know," she asked softly, "that you are my only friend, the only person with whom I can vent my frustration and be my real self? I have not told you how very much I appreciate you. I shall be completely bereft when you are gone."

Justin could not bear to witness her pain. Her anguish seemed a very affront to nature, that one of its most beautiful creations should be in such distress. Before he could warn himself off, before he even realized the import of his words, he found himself making an offer.

"A dandy of a dancing master, eh?" he said lightly. "Well, I am certain those gentlemen can be amusing at times. But if your heart is set upon avoiding one, perhaps I may be permitted to come to your assistance. You may find this difficult to credit, but in certain circles I am considered quite the elegant dancer. Perhaps I might help you brush up your skills."

Felicity leaned forward and placed her small hand on his. "Oh, Justin," she said, smiling in delighted relief, unaware that she had for the first time employed his Christian name, "would you? Oh, it would be such a comfort to me, to have my friend instructing me in the stead of a stranger. And I promise not to unleash my frustration upon you. Well, at the least, not often. Perhaps I could endure this if there is but one person with whom I can be myself."

In the distance, a bell rang, signaling that luncheon would be served imminently. Felicity jumped up.

"Oh, I must change. Look, I have tracked mud all over the carpet. Oh, dear, I am such a terrible housekeeper. Well, I must remember to tell one of the downstairs maids before it is ground in permanently. Please excuse me now. Will I see you at luncheon?"

"Uh, no. I have matters to attend to, and—"

"Well, later, then. And thank you, thank you from the depths of my soul!"

With a slight wave she was gone.

Justin collapsed his head into his hands. Was he raving mad? What manner of man would break his vows to himself so diffidently just because a young woman's tears had moved him to empathy?

Suddenly he sat up straight and drew a deep breath. The die was cast now. He might be a fool, but he had an inner strength awesomely powerful to behold. His task now was to keep that strength as an armor about himself. He could feel empathy for Felicity without falling under her spell. It was merely a matter of will.

Telling himself so, and half-believing it, Justin slowly rose. He suddenly felt the urge for a long neck-or-nothing ride across the countryside to clear his head.

He did not dare to consider the effect Felicity would surely have on him when he put his arms around her to dance.

12

The morning of the race meet dawned in mist, but just before noon the April sun burned through the shroud. With some relief Felicity realized that her new ensemble would not be ruined after all. She still was the target of reproachful glances from Milly for nearly destroying the pink dress.

"What do you think, Nanny?" she asked, pirouetting.

Her gown was a rich golden striped silk trimmed in bright blue. A matching pelisse and parasol completed the ensemble. Small sapphires dangled from her ears, and a fashionable bonnet in gold trimmed with silk bluebells sat perched upon her head.

Nanny surveyed her critically. "Not bad at all. Perhaps ye'll catch a husband at the meet and won't be needin' no fancy ball."

Felicity sighed. She had never dreamed that an ally could be so trying.

From the first moment Felicity had told her of Harriet's plans, Nanny had not hesitated to voice her disapproval. Earl's daughter or no, she contended, all the fuss and nonsense were simply designed to upset her own ordered days. The idea of dozens of guests in the house caused her bottom lip to swell in a formidable pout.

"The ball will be held on a Friday evening," Felicity reminded her gently. "By Sunday afternoon, everyone will have departed."

"And leavin' an unholy mess in their wake, I'll be bound."

Curbing her exasperation, Felicity pointed out, "Well, you will not be responsible for tidying up after them."

"Perhaps not, but the girls will, and won't they be mewlin' about for weeks. And Cook will be right harried, and my tea'll be cold. Mark my words, missy, yer settin' an unholy mess upon us."

Felicity refrained from reminding Nanny that the ball was not her notion, and indeed, were she to have her way, would never take place. She held her hands up as Nanny tugged blue lace gloves onto them.

"Startin' already, the trouble is," Nanny grumbled. "Time was, I put your riding habit on you of a morning and took it off of a night. Perhaps a day dress in between. Now ye're in and out of another dress each time the hall clock chimes."

Her knotted fingers fumbled with the tiny gold buttons. "All fancied up for a horse-race meetin'. Seems to me a sturdy riding habit would suit far better."

When at last the gloves were secured, Felicity breathed a relieved sigh. "Thank you, Nanny. I do not know when I shall return. Perhaps I should ring for Milly to help me undress."

Throwing back her shoulders indignantly, Nanny sniffed. "Hmph. So it's tossin' me out now, ye are. Not good enough to help the earl's daughter. Perhaps ye prefer I just go to the graveyard and lay me down."

"Oh, Nanny." Felicity groaned and turned to her entreatingly. "Please do not bedevil me. I cannot bear all this and listen to your grumbling too."

Nanny peered at her innocently.

"I must go now," Felicity said, shaking her head. Catching up her parasol, she went downstairs.

Her father had ordered up the landau, a carriage scarcely used on an estate where most of the residents preferred riding on horseback. Indeed, Justin and Peter had ridden ahead long ago on their mounts. But on this day Augustus insisted upon the groom walking Emperor slowly to the site of the meet, and he fully intended to travel alongside in the carriage. Only in this manner could Augustus be certain that the groom did not tire Emperor before the main event.

Thus a journey that might have lasted twenty minutes at a fair trot took nearly an hour. Augustus repeatedly halted their progress to calm Emperor. Felicity could not decide who was more skittish, her father or his horse.

But proceeding at such a leisurely pace in the open carriage, with the sun dappling through the leaves and the first blossoms of the apple trees forming, Felicity was not discontent. She had a period of relative quiet in which to think.

Aunt Harriet, once embarked upon her great campaign, had gone forth at a dizzying pace. In an obvious effort to allow Felicity to believe she had some say in the matter, Harriet hounded her constantly with questions about details. Did Felicity prefer roses or lilies to decorate the ballroom? Or would she like a combination of both? In what manner should the ladies' dance cards be designed? Embossed in gold or silver? What menu did she fancy? Which band of musicians? And on and on in an endless flurry of decisions large and small. At first Felicity had determindly answered her aunt, to show at least the spirit of willfulness. But she soon wearied of making decisions and deferred to her aunt, assuring Harriet that she had the utmost confidence in her taste.

Felicity was far from resigned to the notion of marrying.

Attempting time and again to reason with her father, she had met only the most unyielding resistance. Finally he refused to discuss the subject with her. She even had cornered Peter, trying to enlist his aid. He disappointed her with a distracted air that said he could not be bothered; and at any rate, he agreed basically with Augustus. Thus thwarted in her only avenues of persuasion, she had mulled the matter over and concluded that if she exhibited a semblance of cooperation, much less strife would surround her. Left in peace, she eventually might plot an escape from her fate.

At the least she could be grateful that Harriet had departed for London to make arrangements. Her mind freed from the continual demands of Harriet's chatter, she felt much relieved. Yet she still had not arrived at a viable plan.

She first thought of escaping literally. But where would she go? No one she knew would take her in, all being friends or neighbors of her father's. And she could not live on her own, for she had no funds. Any properties to be settled on her would not come to her until her wedding day, just in time to be handed over to her new husband.

Her ideas had taken a more Machiavellian turn, and she had considered coming down with some debilitating disease. But that ploy caused her to shudder, for she would be forced to spend her marriageable years languishing abed, a fate that seemed even worse than being wedded. She had wondered what might happen should she commit one indelicate *faux pas* after another, until no man would have her. But with the properties to be settled on her, some man far down the social scale was bound to ignore her disgrace and offer for her anyway. The situation seemed hopeless.

The one bright light in her days was Justin. Although she blushed to remember her cheek in actually proposing marriage to him, she noted with vast fondness that he had gallantly spared her the humiliation of mentioning it. He had vowed that once the race meeting was over, he would begin her dancing lessons, and she anticipated them eagerly.

She enjoyed her time with him, whether they were arguing vociferously or merely sitting quietly, each absorbed in his own book. But the doom that awaited her hung over Felicity like the executioner's ax, and her happiness was never unclouded.

Still, when they finally arrived at the meadow where the race was to be held, Felicity found herself smiling. Partly her smile stemmed from a contagious excitement among the spectators; partly it was elicited by the sight of Justin, splendidly attired in a black riding jacket with buff-colored trousers and tall silk hat, sitting astride his roan gelding.

He directed the coachman to halt the landau in an advantageous spot, where she would have an unimpeded view of the race. She would have enjoyed strolling about, judging the merits of the other horses with her own educated eye. But her dainty kid boots would never withstand the rigors of a still-damp field, and thus Felicity was confined to the carriage. She told herself glumly that she might as well grow accustomed to restrictions of her freedom.

"Have you gotten a chance to look at the other entrants?" Felicity asked him.

"Yes, Peter and I have had glimpses of them all. Every squire in the county has entered his best animal. It appears the match will be hotly contested."

Felicity frowned slightly. "I still contend that Papa should have brought Khan. Emperor may be more powerful, even faster, but only when he chooses to be. And today he seems uncommonly skittish. Khan simply loves to race, and if given his head, he is as swift as the wind."

Justin grinned at her. "Let us hope so. I have twenty pounds on Khan."

"What!"

"Yes. I finally persuaded your father to sell him to me and to lend me a proficient tiger to ride him. Khan is my entry in the race."

Smiling pertly, Felicity demanded, "Now you have put me in a fine quandary. For which horse shall I cheer?"

Justin tipped his hat to her and bowed from his saddle. "Why, for the winner, of course, milady." Smiling slyly, he kicked his horse into a trot and off he went.

By the time the first race began, the crowd had swelled and enthusiasm buzzed about the meadow course. Khan easily won his heat, as did Emperor. When at last the final race was called, the crowd hummed with anticipation. As the pistol sounded, Felicity found herself standing in the carriage and cheering loudly for both horses. At the finish, Khan crossed first, a neck ahead of their neighbor Henning's gelding. Emperor took a respectable, although disappointing, third place.

After the winners had been presented with their purses, all three of them came over to the landau. Her father's crestfallen face appeared before her in the lead.

"Dammit, Lissie, you were correct after all," he muttered, resigned.

She could not resist a riposte. "You may discover that I am frequently correct in my reasoning, and not solely pertaining to the temperament of horses."

He shot her a frown of reproach, but said nothing further.

"Congratulations," she said to Justin, smiling.

"Thank you. I believe you should have these."

He handed over a large bouquet of daisies tied in yellow ribbons.

"To the victor go the spoils," she protested with a laugh. "That is you."

"And were you not my uncanny tout? I would never have purchased Khan without your glowing recommendation."

Felicity still blushed at the memory of that night at dinner, when she had uttered the unmentionable word "stud." But Justin had teased her without malice, and she laughed as she accepted the flowers.

Henning tipped his hat for her. "Good afternoon, Lady Felicity. Did you enjoy the competition?"

She nodded politely to the man. "I certainly did, Sir Edmund. Congratulations. Your horse made a grand showing."

Henning, a slight man with gingery hair and a ruddy complexion, shrugged in good nature. "Not quite grand enough. But thank you, my dear. I must say you are looking uncommonly lovely today."

Felicity tried to hide her surprise. "Why, thank you, Sir Edmund."

He smiled slightly and, bowing, bade her to excuse him. How curious, thought Felicity, to receive compliments from her father's friend. The last comments Henning had made about her were complaints about her riding through his pastures.

Suddenly she remembered the picnic luncheon, and how Peter had stumbled over his words. She had assumed he had said something he wished he hadn't concerning the race. Now she understood. Peter had also mentioned Lady Henning's death before he glanced guiltily at Justin. So Peter knew about Justin's late wife.

Why had Peter not mentioned her before? And why such a look of abject guilt? Justin had declared himself recovered . . . Felicity shook her head. Peter was ever puzzling to her. Despite great strides toward a more positive attitude, her brother still fell into dark moments. But at least he had made no plans to return to London. As long as he remained in the country, Felicity could hold on to her optimism regarding him.

The men had drifted off to gather in groups and boast about their victories and argue over might-have-beens. One by one the carriages began to roll. They all stopped bidding Felicity good day, asking when they might expect her to call, inquiring about the health of her aunt. Felicity gave polite but short answers, her spirits sinking as each carriage rolled by. She wished with all her heart to be with Augustus and Peter and Justin, looking over the horses and analyzing the race with the grooms.

At long last Augustus rejoined her and they began the journey home. With the exception of a few desultory remarks about the race, they traveled in silence.

The reality of what her life would be like once she was wedded was beginning to wash over Felicity. Her stomach churned each time she imagined it. Now, more than ever, she was determined to avoid her fate. The only question, and an exceedingly perplexing one, was how she would accomplish her escape.

13

Felicity sailed into the ballroom, with Milly and Nanny in tow. Justin was already present, standing at the tall windows that opened to the terrace, gazing out over the formal gardens below.

"Good afternoon," she greeted him gaily. "I am prepared for my examination."

Smiling, he approached her. As ever, she noted, he was impeccably attired, today in a French-blue coat and cream-colored breeches, and a perfectly tied snowy cravat. Early on in the first week of his stay, he had sent to London for his valet and wardrobe, having been traveling unequipped for a long visit when he had happened across Peter at the coaching inn.

"I pray you do not merely boast," he said sternly, but with a jest in his eye. "Remember that I am a strict taskmaster on the dancing floor."

Felicity laughed. "And I am up to the task. Would you mind fetching one of those small tables? I have brought a surprise."

Justin did as she had bidden him, and Felicity called the maid forward.

"Place it on the table, Milly. Carefully, now.'

Aware of the importance of her task, Milly solemnly set a small ornate chest, decorated in gold leaf and painted with pastoral scenes, where Felicity had directed.

"Thank you, Milly. You may go now."

Justin cast a critical eye on the chest. "A handsome piece," he commented. "Austrian design, is it?"

"Yes," Felicity said, pleased. "Peter sent it to me from Belgium some years ago. Now, watch."

She cranked the handle at the side of the chest and then opened the lid, revealing a blue-velvet-lined interior. A delicate tinkling tune wafted on the air.

"It's a musical jewel box," she declared in delight. "And since the tune it plays is a waltz, I thought we might have real accompaniment to our practice today."

They had spent the week following the race meeting going through the precise movements of quadrilles and cotillions. Felicity's only previous experience had been her initiation to the dance from her governess. In truth, it was the only portion of her duties that Miss Marsham had enjoyed, and so they had whiled away many a pleasant hour on the dancing floor. But as quite a few years had passed since Felicity had gone through the movements, she began rather stiffly. Then Justin had suggested she think of the steps as a mathematical pattern, and although the results were not the polished performance she might have wished, she acquitted herself quite creditably.

However, the waltz had not yet been accepted even marginally when first Felicity had learned to dance. Even now, some considered the Austrian import highly improper, especially for unmarried girls. But Aunt Harriet had given reluctant approval to Felicity's learning the waltz, commenting that her niece needed every weapon available in the arsenal were she to snare a prime husband. And then Harriet learned who would be instructing Felicity. Permission to waltz had been mere child's play compared to the awesome difficulty of persuading Harriet to allow Justin to teach her.

Her aunt had turned livid when Felicity announced Justin's offer. Yet, the more implacably Harriet denied her, the more fervently Felicity insisted. The battle had raged on for days, until they had arrived at a tentative truce. Felicity agreed to employ the London modiste to Harriet's choice in the stead of the village seamstress, in exchange for Justin in the stead of a London dance master. The duel had rendered each woman more wary of the other, but Felicity realized that she was far more content with the compromise than Harriet. As a final demand, and one on which she would brook not even the slightest dissent, Harriet decreed that Nanny must be present at all times during the practices. Felicity considered her aunt's overworry regarding propriety to be silly, but she accepted the price she must pay to keep her friend in residence.

She still could not credit Harriet's cold demeanor, indeed, her outright hostility, toward Justin. When she had bluntly questioned her aunt, Harriet had averted her eyes and mumbled that she simply did not care for the man. Felicity wondered how this was possible, since Harriet paid not the vaguest attention nor directed the simplest of conversation toward him, and therefore knew nothing about the man. Still, so relieved was she that Harriet had finally conceded, she cut her inquiries short, remembering Nanny's oft-repeated advice to let sleeping dogs lie.

"Shall we begin?" Justin asked now.

Felicity nodded as Nanny settled into a well-stuffed chair that had been brought into the ballroom for her comfort. The older woman, chary about Justin at first, watched his every move, listened to his every word like a hawk sizing up its prey. But she had been completely taken aback when on the third day he had presented her with a box of French bonbons. She had grumbled rudely about English toffees being good enough for *most* folks, but Felicity noticed how she attacked the sweetmeats with relish and knew that the woman had been charmed to her toes by Justin.

And in truth, Felicity did not mind her presence in the least. Inevitably, within the first fifteen minutes of their practices, Nanny's head would begin to droop and in another few minutes she was snoring softly.

As the music slowed and stopped, Justin commented, "There are no jewels in your chest."

"I removed them before bringing it down. Not," she added wryly, "that I have so many of great value. Somehow, I have never believed that riding habits required the wearing of jewels."

She blinked as a thought occurred to her. "Oh, I nearly forgot to tell you. In this morning's post, I had a letter from Aunt Harriet with the most amazing news. What do you think? The Cleopatra armlet was returned to her!"

Justin raised his eyebrow. "Indeed? I thought it had been among the jewelry stolen by the highwayman."

"It was. The other items were mere trinkets, save one inexpensive but sentimental piece that Uncle Octavius had given her. But the armlet is priceless, and she was sorely distressed to lose it. And then, when she returned to London, she found that a parcel had been delivered in her absence. Imagine her surprise when she opened it to find the armlet. There was no note, and all the servants could remember was that a delivery boy had brought it. Is that not the most curious turn of events?"

Justin agreed that it was, and the incident was forgotten as they began going through the motions of the quadrille.

"This is your final examination," Justin warned. "I shall be strict with the marks I give you."

Felicity concentrated on the intricate movements. When they had finished the pattern, she gazed up at him expectantly. He gave a nod of concession to her proficiency, and Felicity smiled. The cotillion proceeded even more splendidly, and her reward for completion was a wide grin.

"Am I prepared for the waltz now?" she asked.

"I believe you may be. Wind up the music box."

She hurried to crank the tune once more, and returned to her place before him.

"Now," Justin instructed as the music played. "Your left hand rests so upon my shoulder. Very good."

Even through his coat, Felicity could feel his well-muscled firmness. She realized that she had never comprehended how physically powerful he was.

"Now," he continued, "my right hand goes at your back, near the waist, and your right hand goes in mine."

They stood in that pose for a moment. Although during an actual dance, they both would be wearing gloves, their hands for this practice were bare. Felicity felt the warmth of his slightly roughened palm. Her slender fingers were enveloped by his larger, stronger ones.

Justin cleared his throat. "Very well. The rhythm is *one*, two, three . . . *one*, two, three. Do you hear it?"

"*One*, two, three," she repeated, listening. "Yes, I do."

"The first step is long, a bit sliding. The next two, shorter. A mere stepping to the side, actually."

They proceeded slowly. Felicity attempted the move, watching the motion of his feet.

"You must look up at me," Justin told her.

"But then, how should I knnow in which direction to go?"

"Do you feel the slight pressure of my hand at your back?"

His hand rested lightly above her waist. Yet she could feel the strength of it.

"Let that hand guide you," he advised. "With slight pressure, I shall show you the direction."

They made a few attempts, with awkward results.

"Forgive me," Felicity sighed. "I fear I do not understand."

Pursing his lips in thought for a moment, Justin at last said, "Think of it in this manner: when you are riding, especially at a fast pace, you flow with the motion of the horse. Translate that to dancing."

Her eyes widened. "Oh. Yes, I believe I could do that. Let's try, shall we?"

They began swaying to the music, Felicity's head up, concentrating on his hand at her back. Within a few moments she had caught the rhythm, and she smiled brightly.

"Is that it?"

"Yes, indeed. Now we turn."

With Justin guiding, they began whirling about the floor, and after a few turns Felicity abandoned her stiffness for a fluidity that astonished her. She glanced into Justin's eyes, conveying her delight, and he smiled to acknowledge his comprehension.

Looking at him, Felicity suddenly remembered what a handsome man he was. The realization had never struck her with such impact before this. She gazed at the smoothness of his lightly bronzed skin, the glistening softness of his dark, curling hair. His nose was straight and forceful, his chin strong and square. But it was his eyes that captivated her.

They were an umber shade, deeply rich, shaded by dark lashes. A tender glow seemed to emanate from his gaze. She wanted to tumble into that gaze, instinctively knowing that the fall would be sweet and warm and indescribably wondrous.

They were turning more swiftly now, and in an optical illusion, Felicity had the strange sense that they stood still while the ballroom whirled around them. Her heart beat ever faster, until the echo of it drowned out the tinkling of her musical jewel box. She clutched his shoulder more tightly, and her fingers clenched around his. His hand moved more firmly about her waist, nearly encircling it, bringing her to his broad, powerful chest.

Felicity could barely breathe. Her pulse pounded relentlessly in her ears, her cheeks felt flushed, and her very bones seemed to melt into the rhythm of the waltz.

Suddenly Justin stopped, and she swayed dizzily, not trusting her knees to hold her upright. But his strong arm seemed to support her effortlessly, and she knew absolutely no fear of falling.

They seemed suspended in time, neither moving, in breathy silence. Pressed tightly to him, Felicity realized that she could feel his heartbeat too. She was one with him. In the same way that she had sensed the tight connection of their minds, she now felt a vivid physical unity that left her trembling.

Slowly his face moved toward her, and without thinking, she tilted back her head. In the gentlest of motions, Justin brushed his lips against hers. Softly, tenderly, his mouth rested on hers until at last Felicity's bones did indeed seem to dissolve and her knees buckled. Deep in her throat, a small cry sounded.

The sound had the effect of a splash of icy water on Justin. He pulled back abruptly with a horrified expression. She saw him swallow hard as he released her, and she staggered for a moment until she could stand unaided.

For a long moment he stared at her with an expression that caused her first confusion, then dismay, and finally not a little trepidation. His brows were drawn together in a forbidding line, his eyes narrowed, his lips . . . his soft, tender lips . . . straight and pressed tight. She had never seen him like this, appearing so frighteningly angry. His inviting warmth had changed to a dangerous heat before her eyes.

She drew back uncertainly. Then, without a word, he turned on his heel and strode forcefully out of the ballroom.

For a while Felicity stood stock-still, her thoughts hopelessly snarled. She had run the gamut of emotions from tenderness to fear in such a short time, she could not begin to untangle them all. What in the world had happened?

Gradually the reality began to dawn upon her. She had held a man close to her and kissed him. Of all the disgrace that endangered a young lady, this surely was the worst. Belatedly she shot an anxious glance toward Nanny. But thankfully the old woman was sound asleep in her chair.

She knew she should wake Nanny and hurry her from the ballroom in a drowsy state so that the sharp-eyed woman would not suspect anything amiss from Felicity's demeanor. But she did not trust her ability to draw even the flimsiest of veils over her expression, and so she went to sit in a straight-backed chair near to the dozing woman to gather her composure.

All of her upbringing, from Miss Marsham's obligatory lectures to Aunt Harriet's relating of scandalous *on-dits*, had warned against the perils of improprieties. A girl's reputation could be shredded by sins that were merely speculation, not even reality. Felicity realized that she should be aghast at her behavior, based upon this knowledge alone. But privately she did not care a fig about the *haut monde*'s rules. What did upset her was Justin's reaction.

Did he now consider her a fast piece of baggage? She cringed to think that he might judge her harshly. A wave of desolation crashed over her, imagining him turning his back on her figuratively, mimicking what he had done literally.

How could she have jeopardized the only friendship she possessed? On and on she railed at herself, accepting none of her tentative excuses about the spell of the waltz, the spontaneity of the moment. She had committed a towering error in judgment, and had only herself to blame if he cut her dead the next time she saw him.

And yet . . .

Try as she might, Felicity could not erase the rapture of that kiss. The soft, melting tenderness, interlaced with surges of exhilaration. She still recalled in radiant detail the sensation of falling into his velvet gaze, and knew the memory would repose in her mind until the day she died. Her body recognized his embrace as if it were imprinted in her flesh; her spirit remembered her sense of unity with him as if it were seared upon her soul. It seemed as though her emotions regarding Justin were wrapped in a silken affection, but one more powerful than any fondness she had known before.

Felicity reminded herself that since her integration of her true self and her outer self, her feelings had intensified in hue. And still, this vast affection for Justin seemed degrees beyond the usual. What could this signify? She frowned, bewildered.

The answer began as a whispered murmuring in her mind, growing louder and more definite as she listened. *Love?* Had she, Felicity Mariclaire Bellwood, dedicated to the lofty search for intellectual and personal freedom, actually done something so imprisoning as falling in love?

Her mouth fell open in mute astonishment. The very idea was completely preposterous. Yet the more she fought against it, the more decisively the thought lingered. She was in love with Justin Havilland! For a moment she hugged herself and laughed giddily. And then, gradually, the bleak reality of the situation dissolved her laughter.

With great embarrassment she recalled the day she so naively had suggested marriage to him. At the time, her proposal had seemed a mere practicality, a simple answer to avoid her loss of freedom. And while she had accepted his gentle refusal casually then, his words returned to haunt her now.

Felicity knew with a crystalline clarity that he intended never to marry again. He was not "husband material," by his own free admission. And so his kiss was certainly not serious. She had thrown herself at him, and like any virile man, he had succumbed. Her love for him had no path to follow; only a trail of broken dreams awaited her.

And so in the stead of allowing her feelings for Justin to blossom, she must give them no nurturance, stifling her love at its birth.

Her eyes welled with tears that trickled slowly and silently down her cheeks. How unfair of fate, to allow her to feel such glorious emotions only to deny her their full expression. How much better if she had remained in her naive shell and never broken through those damnable walls.

She sniffed back her tears, and beside her, Nanny stirred. Quickly Felicity dabbed at her cheeks with her kerchief and set a determined smile upon her face.

"Eh?" Nanny mumbled, blinking awake. "Oh, there you are, missy. I must have dozed off for a moment. Finished with the lessons, are ye?"

"Yes," Felicity answered softly. "Finished."

Nanny sat up with a pronounced creaking of old bones. "Well, how was it? Did ye trip over yer own feet and disgrace yerself?"

Felicity helped the old woman to rise, then linked her arm through Nanny's.

"I stumbled for a moment," she murmured, steering Nanny slowly toward the door. "But then I righted myself. I will not commit the same mistake again."

"And ain't that a blessing?" Nanny muttered. "Wouldn't do to have ye tumblin' head over hoop in the midst of all them fancy guests yer expectin'."

Felicity stared straight ahead. "No, Nanny. It would not do at all."

14

"*Brush* her down well, Mick," Felicity said to the head groom, handing over Sheba's reins. "I fear I kept her out in the drizzle overlong."

"I'll take care of 'er, milady," the head groom replied in his gravelly voice.

A bit guiltily, she patted the mare, who seemed to whinny in forgiveness. Felicity knew she should not have subjected the horse to such a grueling effort on such a harsh morning. But she was compelled by an urgent need for release that only a long, hard ride could provide.

She had awakened early, and despite the threatening skies, had put on her old riding habit, throwing her hooded cloak about her. The cloak made for a more cumbersome journey, but without it she would have been soaked to the skin within a mile. Now she clutched the folds about herself, ducked her head, and started off for the house.

She had little fear of bumping into Justin this morning. Last evening, still trembling from the afternoon's kiss, she had dreaded facing him. Much to her relief, her father announced before dinner that Justin and Peter had gone into Edgemonton, to the village inn. From Peter's previous visits to the Hound and Hare, Felicity knew that their night had consisted of continual games of draughts, accompanied by bottomless glasses of cheap wine. She doubted that either of them would rise before noon.

Entering through the kitchen garden, Felicity welcomed the warmth of the big iron stove.

"Oh, milady," Cook cooed, espying her. "Let me help ye out of that wet thing afore ye catch yer death."

"Thank you, Cook. I apologize for dripping upon your clean floor, but I feared I would ruin the carpets abovestairs."

"Not to worry," Cook answered cheerily. "Sit at the table, if you please, and let me bring ye a cup of hot tea."

She sent one of the kitchen maids off to fetch an uncracked cup and fussed about Felicity, covering her with a faded lap quilt.

" 'Tis me own," Cook explained, "and many's the rainy day it's kept me cozy."

Felicity accepted the tea gladly, and for a long while she chatted with the woman about her vast family, listening attentively to accounts of weddings and births, and a death or two. Hearing about lives completely disconnected from her own helped Felicity forget her troubles. Finally Cook halted in her chatter, and Felicity looked up to see Dobbs standing reproachfully at the stair.

"Begging your pardon, milady," the majordomo said in his woeful voice. "But 'tis near the luncheon hour—"

"Oh, I'm am sorry," Felicity said, hastily rising and handing back Cook's lap quilt. "The time simply slipped past. I've kept you far too long. Please, go about your business."

Cook sighed a bit regretfully and rose to prepare the luncheon. Felicity waved good-bye, folding her now-dried cloak over her arm, and proceeded abovestairs.

She peered cautiously around the petite foyer and the dining salon. Satisfied that only servants moved about, Felicity sped up the staircase. Condemning herself as a coward, she none-theless could not face Justin at the moment. The upstairs hallway was also deserted, except for the maids. Quietly but swiftly she headed for her room.

Her door was slightly ajar, and she supposed that Milly had gone in to tidy up. But when she entered, she saw an unexpected form bending over her dressing table.

"Peter!" she blurted in surprise.

He spun around toward her and froze. In his fists he clutched her diamond parure.

"Peter," she repeated more softly, a sinking feeling in her stomach.

Avoiding her gaze, Peter straightened. "You might give a body warning," he sniffed bravely. "You like to have frightened me out of my wits."

"I did not realize," she replied evenly, "that I must give warning upon entering my own room. Peter, what are you doing with my jewels?"

He looked simply dreadful. Dark circles once more ringed his eyes and his skin was deathly pale. He appeared to have slept in his shirt, and his unkempt red-gold hair had lost its shine.

Felicity watched him and knew he was dredging his wine-muddied mind for some explanation she might accept. Finally he sighed.

"I would have asked you, if I had found you. But you were nowhere about, and I am in deucedly dire straits."

"So dire," she said, her voice trembling, "that you must help yourself to my diamonds?"

Peter glanced at her sheepishly. "In point of fact, yes."

Her sense of betrayal must have shown in her face, for Peter winced and glanced away.

"Ah, Lissie, please don't chide me so. I would not even have looked to find you, except as a final resort. Please, Lissie."

His gaze was filled with such misery, Felicity at last relented.

"Oh, Peter," she sighed. "What trouble have you gotten yourself into now?"

Shrugging dispiritedly, he murmured, "I fear I had too much wine last night. I lost quite a sum at the inn over draughts."

Felicity stared incredulously. "To the villagers?"

"No. To Henning. We came across him on our way to the inn, and he joined us, worse luck."

"How much did you lose?"

Peter chewed at his lips before replying. "Five hundred pounds," he mumbled at last, reluctantly.

Felicity's eyes widened in disbelief. "Five hundred . . . Peter, are you mad, wagering that amount? What in heaven's name came over you?"

"I don't know, Lissie," he answered dully. "Henning was so dashed smug, and the more I lost, the more smug he became. The entire episode ballooned before I knew what was happening."

"And where," Felicity demanded, her anger smoldering, "was your companion in all this? Why did he not prevent you from making such a fool of yourself?"

"Now, don't blame Justin. In truth, he was further into his cups than I. Still, he did try to dissuade me, but I was in no mood to listen to him. He is not my keeper, Lissie. It's no fault of his that I behaved so stupidly."

Felicity regarded her brother tight-lipped. "God help you, Peter."

Impatiently he approached her. "Very well. You've given me a sound upbraiding, and I have taken it. Now, may we move on to more urgent matters? I told Henning I would have his money for him tomorrow, and he promised not to mention a word of it to Father. I must get to London if I'm to pawn one of your trinkets."

His eyes pleaded with her, and Felicity could not deny him. She closed her eyes for a long moment.

"Very well," she said at last, quietly. "I shall give you one of the diamond ear bobs. If anyone should notice it is missing, I shall confess to having lost it."

"Oh, thank you, Lissie," he exclaimed. Breathing deeply, he peered at her in earnest. "I shall redeem the pawn ticket no later than the end of June, when the half-year rent from the Greenridge estates arrives."

Slowly, with leaden steps, she went to the dressing table and Peter followed her. He opened his hands, and a diamond necklace and bracelet spilled onto the countertop. From a small compartment of the musical jewel box, the very one he had sent to her, she extracted a sparkling ear bob and handed it to him.

From over her shoulder, Peter pointed to the cameo and frowned. "Is that—"

"No," she said decisively, "you may not take my cameo. You gave it to me, and it is my favorite piece."

"Yes," he agreed hastily, "but why break up the diamond parure? I am certain the cameo will fetch enough money, and I'll return it to you—"

"No, Peter," she repeated firmly. Then, wounded, she said, "You cannot take my favorite piece from me."

The effects of the drink must have caught up to him, for he rubbed his hand shakily across his brow. "I don't want it, if it means that much to you. You had better excuse me now, Lissie. I need a hot bath and a gallon of strong tea to put me in shape for the ride to London."

He started across the room; then, at the doorway, he paused, looking back at her. "Thank you, Lissie," he said simply. Turning, he disappeared into the hallway.

Felicity sank into the slipper chair before her dressing table, still clutching her cloak. A chill passed through her and she snuggled into the woolen warmth of the garment.

All her hopeful optimism for Peter lay frozen in that
moment she had discovered him with her jewels. The respite
from his excessive drinking and gaming was over. He had
not changed his destructive ways; he had merely taken a
holiday from them.

Abruptly a flash of anger stabbed at her. War experience
or no, attempting to rob her of her diamonds was unconscionable, dishonorable. And now that she thought upon it,
his demeanor toward her was doubly deceptive: his guilt did
not stem from the act of stealing from her, but from having
been caught at it.

Felicity scarcely could credit this facet of Peter. What other
abominations did he commit to pay for his outrageous
wagering? Had he gone through Papa's room or Aunt
Harriet's . . . ?

Suddenly her heart seemed to stop, and then began beating
again furiously. Oh, no. The idea was too unbelievable, the
premise too scandalous to express. And yet, if Peter were
so desperate as to steal from his own sister . . .

. . . what was to prevent him from raising a pistol and
robbing like a common highwayman?

She jumped up and began pacing frantically about her
room, trying to remember every detail of the day Aunt
Harriet had been accosted on the post road. The clothing the
highpad wore, his horse—neither were familiar to her. But
Peter easily could have rented—or stolen—both in order to
disguise himself. The highwayman's voice had spoken in a
thick Yorkshire accent. But Peter had spent some of his
military training in that area and might have mimicked a
Yorkshireman as another form of disguise.

For every discrepancy Felicity could unearth, her reason
responded with a logical reply. In the robber's escape through
the wood, he had seemed unfamiliar with the path. But that
too might be explained logically. The fleeing high pad had

no cause to think anyone might follow him. He had seen no need for breakneck speed. And why had a cold-blooded highwayman risked identification to save her from being trampled under Sheba's hooves? Only because he had reason particularly to be concerned for her welfare.

Surely, she told herself in desperation, she would have known her own brother, disguised or not. But the events had occurred in such swift motion, her fear had so absorbed her senses, it was entirely possible that she would not have.

And was it not too uncanny a coincidence that Peter chose that very night to arrive unexpectedly for dinner?

The weight of the evidence overwhelmed her, and Felicity groaned in distress. If only there were a way to disprove the theory. Confronting Peter would not grant her reassurance. Sad to say, she felt she could not trust him to be honest with her. Perhaps someone had been with him that day . . .

Justin! Of course. He had met Peter at the coaching inn between London and Edgemonton. With a glimmer of hope, she remembered that Peter had been drunk when he arrived at Bellwood House that evening. Perhaps he and Justin had been drinking at the inn half the day.

With that thought to cling to, Felicity rang impatiently for Milly. Justin would tell her the truth, whatever it might be.

Then she remembered why she had been avoiding Justin and her resolve weakened. Could she face him so soon after yesterday's debacle? Gauging herself, Felicity realized that her need for reassurance about Peter outweighed her trepidation about seeing Justin.

"You rang, milady?" Milly asked, entering the room.

"Yes. Milly, do you happen to know where I might find Sir Justin?"

Milly frowned, ruminating. "Can't say that I do, milady." Then she offered, "I did see him in the hallway a few minutes ago."

"Was he attired for luncheon? Or did he carry his riding crop?"

"No, he had a stack of books in his hands."

"Thank you, Milly . . . Oh, would you mind replacing my jewels? I fear I was sorting through the box . . ."

"I'll tidy up, milady."

Gathering up her skirts, Felicity raced down to the library. She came upon Justin as he was replacing a history of Venice on the shelf.

"Oh, Justin, I am so glad I have found you."

She thought she detected an anxious glint to his gaze when he glanced at her. But then, to her relief, he smiled casually.

"Yes?" he asked in expectation.

"Come, sit with me. I want to ask you something of great importance."

This time she was certain that his eyes held an uneasy glaze. Realizing that he must think she was about to throw herself at his head again, she hastily posed her question.

"The first night you arrived here. Peter said that he had met you at the coaching inn. Was that true?"

His brow wrinkled in puzzlement. "Certainly, it was true."

"When . . ." She inhaled deeply. "When did you first meet him there? At what hour?"

"About five in the afternoon, I suppose. Why do you ask?"

Her heart sank. The robbery had occurred at least an hour beforehand. Peter would have had more than enough time to reach the coaching inn by then.

"But he was so drunk when he arrived here," she protested. "Surely he had been drinking at the inn before then."

He shook his head. "No, actually I arrived before Peter did. I hesitate to mention this, but your brother can become uncommonly drunk in an uncommonly short time. What is all this inquiry?"

Felicity bit her lip, wavering, then plunged into a blurted recitation of her suspicions, a list of the mounting evidence that led her to worry that Peter was the highwayman.

When she was finished, Justin brushed a hand at her fears. "All your theories are circumstantial. There is no proof in your logic."

"But the coincidence of arriving here hours later . . ." she objected.

"That was no coincidence," Justin said bluntly. "We had agreed to meet at the inn, as your brother always stops there to fortify himself when coming in from London. Peter mentioned that he had merely 'happened' to come across me so that he would not have to reveal to his father the real reason for his visit. He had lost a great sum of wagers to me, and offered a pair of horses to settle the debt. There was no coincidence."

"Truly?" she asked, weak with relief.

"Truly," he assured her. "Whatever encouraged you to create this absurd theory in the first place?"

Felicity averted her gaze. "Oh, I expect it was the product of my fancy. What a goose I was."

"Well, I am delighted that I was able to set your fancy back on solid ground." Justin rose. "If you will excuse me now, I must see to my valises."

Felicity glanced up in surprise. "Your valises?"

"Yes," he answered diffidently. "I am departing for London this afternoon."

Her spirits, puffed to such heights when he had dismissed her fears regarding Peter, suddenly collapsed. "You are leaving?"

"Yes, I must go. I have neglected my own matters far too long, I fear. Not," he added politely, "that I have not enjoyed your hospitality immensely."

Felicity got to her feet swiftly. "Oh, Justin, please stay," she said in a rush, without thinking, clutching at his arm.

"I am sorry about yesterday. I do not know what madness came over me, but I apologize and I promise never to repeat such disgraceful behavior. I cannot bear the thought of your not being here."

"Felicity," he said, gently disengaging her hand, "you are not to blame for my horrific actions of yesterday. I accept total responsibility for taking so unconscionable a liberty with you. It's I who must beg your forgiveness for a moment of inexplicable madness."

Somehow, his words did not so much relieve as disappoint her.

"Well, then," she said stiffly, "let us simply put the situation behind us, forget that it ever occurred, and go on as friends."

"I cannot forget," he said so softly Felicity had to strain to hear him. Then, in a stronger voice, he added, "I believe it best that I go. Your aunt will be returning soon, and you will be occupied night and day, at any rate. You will not even notice that I am gone."

"Oh, I will notice," she vowed in a low, ardent tone. "I will miss you dreadfully."

For a moment she merely looked at him, her heart brimming with words that must always remain unspoken. Then Felicity attempted a bright smile.

"But until I see you again, I shall employ my time in strengthening my knowledge of ancient Greece. I shall eventually prove to you, for once and for all, that Agamemnon, even though mythical, possessed a far superior military mind to that of Alcibiades."

Justin smiled and bowed slightly. "I accept your challenge. But forwarned, I too shall brush up on my studies."

Felicity paused, holding back her tears. "*À bientôt*, Sir Justin," she murmured.

"Farewell, Lady Felicity," he replied.

She whirled and ran from the room.

15

The lazy afternoon warmth of June encompassed Felicity. She stirred on her chaise longue, realizing that she had, indeed, fallen asleep for a short while. Aunt Harriet had insisted upon a midday nap as a hedge against the rigors of the upcoming evening. And while Felicity privately felt more skittish than Emperor on his worst day, apparently her exhaustion had won out over her nerves.

The day she had dreaded was finally at hand. Tonight was her come-out ball. And the preparations for it had been as trying as the event itself was sure to be.

In late April, not long after Justin had departed, Aunt Harriet arrived back at Bellwood House, twittering and cheerful. The arrangements were unfolding more smoothly than even she had hoped, and now Felicity must join in the proceedings.

The modiste, along with a dozen assistants, arrived first. They set up shop in the old nursery, for the sewing room was far too small to accommodate all of them, plus the bolts of fabric, the miles of ribbon, the boxes of thread and needles they brought. Felicity had spent hours being prodded, pinned, and tucked, and her mind swam with color choices for days.

Then the team of workmen arrived and swept through the house like a plague of locusts, tearing off old wall coverings and pasting up new, refitting chairs and settees, rehanging window draperies. When they were finished, another team of footmen on loan from Lady Ashford helped the household servants scrub and polish the seldom-used guest wing, gradually moving on to the rest of the house. For weeks the smell of soap and beeswax greeted Felicity wherever she went. From Milly she learned that those in regular service at Bellwood House wavered between grumbling indignantly about the lack of confidence in their abilities, and sighing in secret relief that the Ashford Hall servants also were working their fingers to the bone, sparing to some degree the appendages of the resident staff.

After that, the parcels began to arrive; and not the usual discreetly tied packages, but huge crates. In them were new linens and blankets, candleholders and chamber pots, jars of jams and chests of rare teas; a veritable cornucopia of household goods.

And then there were Aunt Harriet's lists. Felicity vowed that the stack of them would reach the ceilings (which all had been replastered, causing Felicity to sneeze from the dust for a month). She was asked to make so many decisions that finally she merely pointed at random, simply to finish the task.

She rarely saw her father. When she did, he was inevitably flexing his fingers, either figuratively or literally, to relieve the cramping he suffered from signing so many accounts for payment by his banker in London. She begged Mick to be certain to exercise Sheba, for heaven only knew when, if ever, she would have the time for a ride on her mare again.

Georgina had arrived early in May and had eagerly thrown herself into the fray. Felicity was ever grateful, for not only did Georgina make some of the choices for her, but her cousin's presence gave Aunt Harriet another target for her endless nattering and complaining.

All in all, Felicity's spirit had been depleted near the middle of May. And Aunt Harriet had waited until then to spring the most fearful trap upon her.

It seemed that, before her come-out ball, she must be presented at court. Felicity had gone into a fit of protest, but Harriet must have expected such, for she merely remained silent until Felicity grew weary of the battle. It was decided that, time being of the essence because the London Season was nearly over, Georgina's court dress should be refashioned to fit her. When Felicity saw what she was expected to wear, she laughed until the tears rolled down her cheeks. Easily the most ridiculous gown she had ever laid eyes upon, it was made of heavy white satin overlaid with silver tulle and furbelow, high-waisted *à la haut ton*, but with a wide hoop at the hem. No fewer than a dozen white ostrich feathers soared upward in a plume from the headpiece, a circlet of white roses and pearls.

When she had ceased her laughing, Aunt Harriet made her put on the gown and practice curtsying thus attired until Felicity thought she would drop. The day before the big event, they all had traveled to Harriet's London town house. When the moment was finally upon her, Felicity had been so racked with nerves, her teeth chattered. Afterward she could remember not one minute of the ordeal, from the time she stepped warily from the carriage until she was back in it again. Apparently she had comported herself passably, for Aunt Harriet beamed for three days.

Yesterday, the guests had begun arriving. As she had not been officially presented to the *ton* yet, Felicity was not expected to greet any of them, or even to take her meals with the rest of the family. The happiest moment she had known in months was when Harriet apologetically informed her that she would be confined to her room until she appeared at the ball.

So for two days she had listened through her open windows to the continual noise of arriving carriages grinding on the gravel drive, the tittering of women that resembled the chirping of demented birds, and the hearty harrumphing of gentlemen shouting greetings as if they had not seen each other in years, rather than hours. After a while, she slammed shut the windows; but the heat weighed on her so oppressively that she finally relented, opened them again, and stuffed her ears with cotton wool.

Thus protected, and wholly exhausted, Felicity had fallen into a restless sleep upon her chaise longue.

Now she saw by her mantel clock that at any moment she could expect Milly and Georgina and Harriet and any of her cronies who cared to watch the grand show of dressing her.

And tonight was but the beginning. Felicity feared that she never would be afforded another moment's solitude for the rest of her life. No magical plan had occurred to her, no rescue from her fate. And in truth, since Justin had departed, so had much of her spirit. She could not seem to muster up any rebellion. Feeling a sudden melancholy, Felicity reached for her secret journal, hidden under the pillow. It had grown to quite a sizable number of entries, no surprise considering that she had had much to spill out onto the pages.

Reading portions here and there, she noticed with a wry nostalgia how naive she sounded in the first passages. So exhilarated about the unveiling of her true self. That inner person had scurried back behind the walls months ago, when Harriet had first returned. Her aunt had caught Felicity in the library rereading Homer, turned white, and gasped that she would expire on the spot if ever the word got out that Felicity was a socially disastrous, a totally odious *bluestocking*.

When she came to the passages regarding Justin, Felicity felt a wounding pang and closed the book abruptly. Not a day ticked by without her thoughts centering upon him a dozen times, the memory always accompanied by an ache that refused to release her. She closed her eyes and slipped the journal back under her pillow.

Only a few minutes later, the knock sounded at her door. She could hear out in the hallway the chattering voices of Aunt Harriet and Georgina and other, unidentified females. Sighing, Felicity took a deep breath and called, "Enter."

She had been standing in the receiving line for hours, and was certain that she had been introduced to every last resident of London and some persons who were just passing through. Although she positively knew she would not recall one name, Aunt Harriet seemed well-acquainted with them all. Felicity had had no idea that one woman could have twenty or thirty "dearest friends."

Finally the last guest went through the line and Aunt Harriet pulled her aside.

"Felicity, dear, trot on off to the ladies' receiving room and press a wet cloth to your face. While a bit of color in the cheek is charming, you are quite flushed."

"Small wonder," Felicity mumbled. "I vow it is warm enough in here to cook an egg."

"For the love of heaven, Felicity, erase that frown. Nothing will ruin your chances more quickly than the perception that you possess a sour disposition. Now, run off before the dancing begins. But do not actually run. Glide. And *smile*."

Smiling, gliding, Felicity slipped away from her aunt. But she did not go to the reception room. She headed to the library and slipped outside.

She could hear some of the guests around the corner, at the other end of the terrace. But she stood in the shadows, hoping they would not venture this far.

She wished she could find the smallest pleasure in this tribulation. She knew that her gown was lovely. The fluttering white silk, shot with golden threads, was soft and graceful. She had insisted that the trimmings be made in willow green, so that she had an excuse to wear her cameo in the stead of the diamonds that Aunt Harriet had decreed *de rigueur*. Perhaps as a peace offering after the ordeal of the court presentation, her aunt begrudgingly had agreed. She actually had sent the brooch to London, so that replicas of it could be made into ear bobs and even a golden tiara set with miniatures of the cream-and-pale-green cameo.

The brooch now hung delicately from a gold chain about her neck. Felicity carefully detached the cameo and held it tightly in her hand, fancying it a talisman to prevent her inevitable fate.

A slight movement distracted her and she turned to see a man quietly standing a few feet away, regarding her. As he stepped closer, into the light shining out from the library, she gasped.

"Justin!"

He was tall and impossibly handsome in his evening clothing. Smiling, he gave a slight bow.

"Am I addressing the new toast of London?"

Felicity laughed in delight. "I cannot believe that you came. You did not reply to the invitation."

"A grave social error for which I apologize. I take it I am welcome regardless?"

She came forward and touched his sleeve to assure herself that it was really he who stood before her, and not some phantasm of her most fervent wishes.

"Of course you are welcome. More than welcome. I think that I have never been so glad to see anyone in my entire life."

"Still hedging about your thoughts, I see," he commented

dryly. Pausing a moment, he added softly, "You are a vision of beauty, you know."

"I am?" she asked, inordinately pleased.

He shook his head in mock reproach. "Careful, Lady Felicity. The first rule of the *haut monde* is that a comely young woman should never fish about for compliments. She must flutter her eyes behind her fan and wait for paeans to her charm to come flowing forth spontaneously."

"Oh, bother the rules. I have been drilled with rules until I am blue-faced."

"Quite a trial, all this, hmm?"

"Oh," Felicity replied fervidly, "you have no notion. It boggles the mind."

Off around the corner, she heard the sounds of the musicians tuning their instruments in the ballroom.

"Oh, no," she groaned, disappointed. "If I am not back to lead the first quadrille with Papa, Aunt Harriet will strangle me with her ruby necklace. Are you coming inside?"

"Perhaps in a few minutes."

"Splendid." Felicity remembered the cameo in her hand and refastened it to the neck chain. "Then I shall see you later? Justin?"

But he acted as if he had not heard her. He was staring fixedly at the brooch.

"Where did you get that?" he asked, his voice brusque.

"What, the cameo?" Bewildered by his abrupt change in tone, she peered at him questioningly. "Peter gave it to me two years ago. Why?"

His face had gone as white as his cravat. With a tremulous smile he attempted to recover himself. "It is . . . such an unusual piece. One seldom sees cameos set on pale green backgrounds."

But Felicity knew that somehow the brooch had disturbed him mightily. Before she could query him further, the beginning notes of the quadrille issued forth on the night air.

"I truly must go," she said urgently. "But please stay and talk with me later. Please give me one small piece of tonight that I may enjoy."

Justin nodded wordlessly, and although Felicity loathed leaving him in this manner, she hurried over the terrace to the corner, pausing only to wave briefly.

"Until later?" she called.

But she could not wait for his reply. Swiftly she hurried toward the open doors leading to the ballroom.

Justin managed to remain upright until she had disappeared around the corner. Then he leaned heavily against the wall, breathing slowly, attempting to recover his equilibrium.

The sight of the cameo brooch had turned his blood to ice. So totally unexpected, to catch a glimpse of it dangling on a chain about Felicity's neck. And Peter had given it to her! For a moment Justin's anger raged like a wild beast inside him. The bald nerve of the cad!

Justin had known he should not come here tonight. It was a mistake, the likes of which would haunt him for years.

When he had left Bellwood House in April, he could not wait to put the miles between him and Felicity. After that insane episode in the ballroom, he could not afford to be in her presence for one moment longer.

He truly had thought that he must have teetered on the edge of lunacy. To pull her close to him in the waltz, in a brazen embrace, and then actually to have kissed her! Besides ranging far beyond the pale of propriety, his behavior had been nothing short of the first spark to self-immolation.

But the feelings that had prompted his action still glowed in his memory. The creamy perfection of her skin, the coppery sheen of her hair, the faint scent of rosewater hovering about her, all had combined to fan the embers resting secretly in his heart. He had clasped her to his chest without thinking, only feeling an instinctual need to have her heart beat next to his own. Her soft pink lips had attracted him magnetically, and he had pressed them with his own as if drawing from her the very breath of life itself.

The horror of what he had done had begun to dawn on him only as he had pushed her away. Only later, at the village inn and well on his way to a monumental drunkenness, had the true import of his deed struck him.

He was making the same disastrous error with Felicity as he had with Alice. With his wife, the passions had been an August storm, dark and sultry, lightning bolts of fascination with torrential and primal rains that had nearly drowned him. With Felicity, the desires were a spring afternoon, hypnotically warm and deceptively peaceful, sunlight and gurgling brook and a circlet of wildflowers that could ensnare him a nefariously as an iron chain.

Both women were lethal to him, Felicity merely more subtly and therefore more dangerously so. For she was the most treacherous form of Bellwood: an intelligent one. He had thought he could contain his emotions around her by matching her considerable wits and keeping himself in strict control. How dismally wrong he had been.

So why had he come here tonight? When the invitation had arrived at his London town house, he had ripped it to shreds and thrown it away. But not before memorizing the date. As late as this afternoon, Justin had entertained no notion of attending the come-out ball. But after pacing restlessly through his entire house, he had abruptly ordered his valet to pack his evening clothes and set off at a swift pace, booking a room at the coaching inn. Returning to Bellwood House like a moth to a flame.

Justin had told himself that he wanted to see Felicity one last time, assuring himself that his desire stemmed from simple curiosity. Would she go through the motions and enter society? Or had she plotted some escape?

When he had seen her standing so small and alone on the terrace, his heart had quivered at her vulnerable beauty and wrenched with chagrin that she had not eluded her fate. He had felt a gathering urgency to wrap his protection around her and whisk her away. Remembering the moment now, Justin suddenly caught his breath.

My God, he thought in dismay. I have fallen in love with her.

His feeling for Felicity had such a different quality from the "love" for Alice that had possessed him that he had not recognized its true meaning. Or perhaps he had known from the first, and simply refused to own to it.

His shoulders sagged a bit as he realized that it mattered little either way. The final reality was that the situation was impossible. He could not bolster his love to fruition; he could not marry Felicity. Augustus would never permit such a union. Neither would Justin's own honor.

Could he afford one final waltz with her if he swore an oath to himself never to see her again? He imagined his arm at the waist of her ethereal white gown, her azure eyes gazing up to him, her smooth skin gleaming in the candlelight . . .

. . . and the cameo brooch resting upon her bosom.

Justin rubbed at his suddenly throbbing temples. He thought himself adept at masking his true feelings. But with that cameo brooch mocking him, the brooch that her own brother had given her, Justin knew that he could not pull off such a charade.

Slowly, with the ballroom music floating in his ears, Justin turned and walked away.

16

"Felicity, please!" Aunt Harriet muttered through gritted teeth. "Sir Charles spoke to you for five minutes without your hearing a word he said."

For the hundredth time that evening, Felicity's gaze scanned the ballroom. "Hmm?"

"Felicity!"

Harriet's emphatic growl finally caught her attention.

"I beg your pardon, aunt?"

Sighing deeply, Harriet replied, "Are your social talents so meager that I must remind you to listen when someone speaks to you?"

Felicity shrugged. "He merely was reciting an account of the last seventeen soirees he had attended. I thought I should expire from boredom."

"Boredom? However can you be bored by a man with an income of thirty thousand a year?"

Felicity grimaced in distaste. "Is it not terribly rude that you are privy to that information?"

"Is it not terribly stupid that you do not consider it significant?" Harriet snapped back.

They stared at each other for a moment. Then Felicity felt the tension between them easing.

"Please forgive me, Aunt Harriet. I am frightfully skittish this night."

"As I am also. Let us simply put it aside, shall we? If you cannot bring yourself to speak to these gentlemen, at the least smile and pretend you are listening."

To Felicity it seemed she had been doing precisely that all evening. After a while, their faces and voices had blended into one generic whole, and she could spot no differences between Viscount This and the Earl of That.

Worse, she had not seen Justin since those few minutes on the terrace. Time and again she had peered through the vast ballroom, but in vain. Surely she could not miss him, tall and handsome and radiating masculine strength in his evening attire. Once more she glanced around, only vaguely noticing the immaculate gentlemen all clothed in formal black twirling ladies in bright-colored gowns, the light from a thousand candles glittering in their jewels and glowing in the banks of white roses and lilies against the walls.

One of the gentlemen now stood in front of her, obscuring her vision.

"Lady Felicity, I believe that is our dance."

She sighed. At least this was a familiar one. "Yes, Sir Edmund, I believe you are correct."

Offering his arm, he escorted her onto the dancing floor. Edmund Henning waltzed passably well, resting his hands upon her as if she were made of delicate glass. His pace was gentle enough to permit conversation.

"You are a lovely credit to your family, Lady Felicity," Henning said.

"Why, thank you, Sir Edmund."

"Before now, I had known you only as a child, riding hither and yon about the countryside. Certainly you are grown to a beautiful woman now."

"Sir Edmund, you flatter me excessively."

"No, no," he assured her solemnly. "Every word I speak is true. You are quite the most comely young lady I have ever seen."

Tiring of his exaggerated compliments, Felicity thought to turn the conversation to lighter, more neutral topics. "I credit my good health to the clean country air. Do you also enjoy the country?"

"Oh, yes. I rarely venture beyond the estate. But surely such a charming young lady as you prefers the gaiety of London."

"Oh, no," she contradicted firmly. "I should happily live out my days in a place just like Bellwood House. You must be a man of rare good taste if you, too, prefer the peacefulness of your estate to the frenzy of London."

Henning smiled, and his inherently florid complexion reddened the more. Apparently he had decided that his conversational duties toward his neighbor's daughter were satisfied, for he completed the waltz in a blessed silence and returned her politely to her aunt's side.

"Thank you, Lady Felicity."

"It was my pleasure, Sir Edmund."

The moment he was gone, Harriet grabbed at Felicity's wrist and peered at her gold-etched dance card.

"What is next? Ah, a cotillion. And with Viscount St. John! Oh, Felicity, he is a splendid catch. Heir to the Earl of Tremont, and possessing no outrageous vices, to the best of anyone's knowledge. Please, please, make an effort with him, Felicity. And for the love of heaven, do not stare at his crossed eyes."

Felicity gave her a weary smile. "I shall be the soul of discretion."

As she waited for the splendid catch to arrive, Felicity noticed Peter, who had not danced since the obligatory quadrille with his sister, leading a pert dark-haired young miss onto the dancing floor.

"Who is that with Peter, Aunt Harriet?" Felicity asked with some interest.

"Where? Oh. That is Lady Sarah Sumner, daughter of Lord Wentham. She was at the court presentation with you, do you not recall? I attended her come-out last month. They did not have half so many flowers as you, and the roast beef at supper was dried out."

Felicity watched intently for a moment. The two were deep in conversation and her brother appeared to be enjoying himself immensely with the pretty Lady Sarah. When he noticed Felicity smiling at him from the sidelines, Peter waved and grinned like a schoolboy on holiday. Hope flickered in Felicity. Perhaps all Peter needed to turn his life about was a sufficiently good reason to give up his wine and gaming quests.

Before she could speculate further, another gentleman bowed before her. Fixing her gaze on a spot above his nose, Felicity murmured, "Good evening, Viscount St. John. Yes, indeed, this is your dance."

On and on the evening dragged, until Felicity's feet ached from dancing and her face numbed from smiling. And still Justin had not appeared. With every dance, her spirits sank the more, until, when the final waltz began, she was completely despondent. To Harriet's consternation, she begged off her partner, turning to her aunt with pleading eyes.

"I cannot bear one more step of dancing!"

"Felicity," Harriet said urgently under her breath, "this is the last one. With Lord Rogers, son of the Duke of—"

"I do not care if he is the son of the king. My feet cannot move another inch. If I attempt to dance, I shall fall flat on my—"

"Very well, Felicity," Harriet replied hastily. "I shall make your apologies to Lord Rogers."

Impulsively she hugged her niece, surprising them both.

"You have comported yourself in an exemplary manner, my girl. With a bit of luck, you shall be the toast of London before the week is out."

"At the moment," Felicity said tiredly, "I should be delighted to be the first person asleep at Bellwood House."

Within fifteen minutes, her wish was fulfilled.

Felicity could not have said what precisely had disturbed her sleep. Whether she had heard a noise or felt a presence was not clear. But one moment she had been deep in slumber, and the next she was wide-awake and sitting up in her bed.

The moonlight streamed through the open windows, illuminating the room well enough. With a catch in her breath, Felicity noticed a form bent over her dressing table.

Not again, she thought miserably. Oh, Peter.

Silently she turned back the coverlet and slipped on her dressing gown. Barefoot, she padded soundlessly across the room.

"What jewel are you searching for now?"

The form straightened at the sound of her voice. But the moonlight glinted on dark hair, not red-gold.

"Justin, what are you doing here?" she nearly screeched.

His answer was soft, ironic. "Ruining your reputation, unless you lower your voice."

She peered at him, bewildered, but obligingly spoke in a quieter tone. "I do not understand. What are you doing in my room, in my jewel box?"

Justin regarded her for a moment. Finally he shrugged. "Precisely what I appear to be doing. Stealing your jewels."

"What!"

"Well, not your jewels, plural. Just one of them."

He held up his hand and the cameo brooch gleamed softly in the dim light.

"But . . . but why?"

Waving his hand diffidently, he replied, "Why does anyone steal jewels? Perhaps I need the money it will bring at pawn."

"If you need money, why did you not simply ask me?"

"Perhaps my pride would not permit it. We males are a notoriously proud species. Or perhaps I steal for the mere pleasure of it. Perhaps it is quite an exciting occupation, slipping undetected into houses that do not belong to me, filching bright, shiny objects. Perhaps—"

"Oh, do cease with your 'perhaps,' " she said angrily. "I care nothing for your intellectual speculations. Tell me the truth."

"I have told you," he countered. "Yours is not the first lady's boudoir into which I have stolen at three o'clock in the morning. Yours is not the first jewel box through which I have rifled."

She stared at him stupefied. "But why?"

Again, that ironic tone. "The ordinary vices of drinking, gaming, and flirtations can be so costly. The vice of stealing jewels pays its own way."

Felicity's knees felt suddenly weak, and she edged awkwardly onto the slipper chair. "Oh, I scarcely can credit that I am hearing this from you. You call robbery a mere vice? It is a crime. It is . . . dishonorable."

"Is it always?" he asked with interest. "What if I had good reason to steal? What if I were taking jewels from people who care very little for them, and give them to people who feed their children from the proceeds?"

"Justin, please," she said quietly. "Do not attempt to confound me with moral dilemmas. The fact is, for whatever reason, you are not the man I thought you to be. You steal! As a source of funding, as a pleasurable pastime, as a noble gesture . . . It makes no difference. How long have you been at this?"

His mouth curved in a tight smile. "Somewhat more than a year."

"So for more than a year," Felicity said incredulously, "you have been robbing ladies of their jewels! And to think that I was so aghast at Peter, looking for one tiny ear bob. I am simply . . ."

Suddenly she halted and her breath came out in a gasp.

"It was *you* who robbed Aunt Harriet. *You* are the highwayman!"

She stared at him, horrified. Justin stood silently, unmoving, making no attempt to disclaim her accusation.

"Oh, yes," Felicity said grimly, "all the evidence that I thought pointed to Peter fits you perfectly. You arrived at the coaching inn long before Peter, you admitted as much. Perhaps you were there when Aunt Harriet passed by, and seeing her put the idea in your head. Oh, it must have seemed exciting to you, enjoying your 'vice' on the open road, in broad light of day. You were not riding your roan, of course. Someone at Bellwood House would have recognized the horse later. So you hired—or stole—a fresh horse and a change of clothing.

"And," she went on relentlessly, "you were in the same regiment, at the same military training ground in Yorkshire, as Peter. Mimicking that accent would come as naturally to you. I was correct in my first assessment: you proceeded slowly on the path through the wood because you were unfamiliar with it." She paused, indignant. "Well?"

Justin shrugged. "I have nothing to add. You have all the answers."

"Oh, yes?" she challenged him. "There is one I do not have, so forgive me if I must look to you for a reply. Why did you stop Sheba? Why did you not simply allow me to be trampled under her hooves?"

His shrugging was driving her mad. "The latent gentleman

in me, I suppose. I have no qualms about taking a lady's jewels. I am not so cavalier about her life."

"How gallant of you," Felicity remarked scathingly. "Now, permit me another question. Why did you return the Cleopatra armlet?"

"I never knowingly take a lady's heirloom pieces."

"And how do you know whether or not a piece is an heirloom?"

"In the circles from which I steal, the provenance of almost every jewel is public knowledge. Ladies are forever nattering on about family pieces. These pieces of which they never speak are the ones I take."

Justin paused expectantly, seeming to await her next query. But Felicity was suddenly weary to her bones. This could not possibly be the same man she loved. And yet, he claimed to have been robbing for more than a year. Why had she not sensed such a major quirk in him?

"If you are finished with your inquiry," Justin said now, almost politely, "I shall go. I can depart in one of two manners. You may scream yourself blue and bring the entire household down upon me, in which case your father will undoubtedly march me off to the authorities with his pistol at my back. That is, if he does not simply shoot me first.

"Or you may sit there silently and protect your reputation while I slip out with no one the wiser. The choice is yours."

Felicity actually opened her mouth to scream. But just as abruptly, she pressed her lips together. She was so stunned, so wounded by his admissions, she had not even the energy to move.

"I believe your decision is a prudent one," Justin said in that same unemotional, maddeningly detached tone. He might have been discussing whether she preferred tea or chocolate for breakfast.

He began to leave.

"Wait!" Felicity snapped. "Give me my cameo brooch."

Justin hesitated, and for the first time since she had discovered his presence, he showed some emotion.

His mouth curved bitterly, and he tossed the brooch onto her dressing table. Without another word, without another sound, he crossed her room and slipped out to the hallway.

Surely, Felicity told herself as she climbed back into her bed, this was all a horrid dream. In the morning, she would awaken to find her cameo resting where it always had, inside a special compartment of the musical jewel box. Somewhat relieved, she drifted back to sleep.

But in the clear, sunny light of the following day, she found the brooch resting carelessly on her dressing table.

Exactly where Justin had tossed it.

17

The summer was two-thirds over, the loveliest edition of the season anyone could remember for years. The rains seemed to fall only when the fields thirsted, the crops promised a record yield, and game was abundant in the woods. A lazy cheerfulness swept through the countryside, inspiring more house parties, fishing parties, and daily visiting than even the eldest of the dowagers had ever seen before.

And one head more toasts to the health of a certain Lady Felicity Bellwood than to anyone else, save the king. She was a diamond of the first water, it was generally agreed, and who could have predicted it? Queer lot, those Bellwoods, with the odd sudden death of the last earl, and the current earl, *on dit*, all but sleeping in the stables. Indeed, one never knew how bloodlines wound out. That was what made for exciting horse races.

On an afternoon in early August, the focus of all this admiration was seated on a shaded bench in the garden at Bellwood House, watching the gardeners clipping the hedges and topiary shrubs. The sound of their shears, rhythmical and precise, had a soothing effect upon Felicity, as did the gardeners' avid concentration on each minuscule portion of the shrubbery. One small twig, one tiny leaf out of place, and *snip*! went the shears, restoring smooth shapes and neat lines to the topiary hedges.

In essence, Felicity had been engaged in the same pursuit for the entire summer. She could not bear to look at the whole of her life, stretching on endlessly. So she snipped at a leaf here, and learned to listen with only one ear to the insipid gossip of the ladies she and Harriet visited. She clipped at a twig there, and realized that she was not required to answer the gentlemen's effusive compliments so long as she smiled slightly at them.

The outer effect was the same one she had projected for years. But the inner effect was far different. Whereas before, her mind was continually churning, judging this statement total rubbish, and that statement one she could refute in two sentences, and inwardly raging at the injustice that forced her to keep silent, Felicity now closed her mind down entirely. She would not permit herself to think even one lucid thought, for thinking brought memory, and memory was the most painful injustice of all. Her mind remained a blank cipher.

The gardeners had finished their work, and with tips of their caps to her, strolled off to the shed. Opening her parasol, Felicity slowly rose and walked back toward the house, one foot in front of the other, a task she could manage without too much effort. In a few minutes, Harriet would summon her, for it was Thursday, her aunt's visiting day while in the country. Paying calls was not such a chore. She could thank her hostess for the cup of tea and delicate sweetmeats, inquire after her health, and then sit back and take a mental nap, with only a nod or a shake of her head and an occasional "Indeed? Do tell," required of her.

"There you are, Felicity dear," her aunt sang out gaily now as Felicity came round the house to the waiting carriage.

"And how lovely you look in that costume! Bishop's blue, I believe that shade is called. It sets off your hair to perfection. Come along, now. We must not keep Lady Ashford waiting."

With the aid of the footman, Felicity obediently climbed into the open landau, tilting her parasol against the warmth of the sun. Harriet patted her arm and smiled fondly at her niece.

Since the day after her come-out, Aunt Harriet had been pleased beyond measure. That morning, with Felicity still stunned by the recognition of Justin's true colors, Harriet had sailed excitedly into her room, rhapsodizing about the brilliant triumph Felicity had scored the previous evening. As evidence, Harriet had confided, bouquets of floral tribute were arriving, eventually to number more than thirty. And before noon, tribute of a different ilk, in the form of six potential suitors, had already come to call, leaving their *cartes de visite* for her to peruse later.

Harriet derived great enjoyment from speculating over who the fortunate winner of Felicity's hand might be. She had raised her expectations considerably, declaring that nothing short of an earl, or an heir who would eventually become one, would have a chance in this matrimonial sweepstakes.

When her aunt prodded Felicity to reveal her special favorites among the suitors, Felicity employed the same diverting trick that worked so well on the gentlemen who pursued her. She smiled vacuously, then raised her fan and looked delicately away. Harriet was delighted, the mystery of who the object of Felicity's *tendre* could be adding spice to the game.

On this particular afternoon, Lady Ashford's drawing room was filled with various ladies and gentlemen whose faces and voices Felicity was beginning to know vaguely. She chose a seat next to Sarah Sumner, whom Felicity genuinely liked.

Sarah was more interested in upcoming soirees and the latest fashion plates in *La Belle Assemblée* than Felicity ever would be. But she found Sarah's *joie de vivre* charming, and realized that the girl was no wet goose. She had a sparkling wit and a generous nature, and Felicity was becoming rather fond of her. To her private gratification, Peter had spent more time that July at the Sumner estate than at his own.

"Felicity!" Sarah said now. "How lovely you look."

Felicity smiled. "And may I return the compliment?"

"Thank you, darling girl. I had to travel all the way to London last week for a fitting of this costume. My modiste refuses to come to the country. Can you credit such cheek? But she is a magician, I must own, and well she knows that I would sooner wear rags than dismiss her." Pausing, Sarah then bit her lip shyly. "And how is your dear brother faring?"

"You would know better than I," Felicity said wryly.

Sarah tapped her anxiously with her fan. "Oh, hush, Felicity. If Lady Ashford should hear you, she will watch me like a falcon at her next house party. I shall have not a moment to speak to Peter without her sticking her pointy nose into the conversation."

Even now, she peered about to reassure herself that neither Lady Ashford nor any of the other dowagers had overheard. Finally satisfied, she turned back to Felicity.

"Have you heard? There is to be a masquerade ball at that house party. What delicious fun! I think I shall dress as a Dresden shepherdess . . . Will you be attending?"

"I am not certain. Aunt Harriet makes all the decisions on whether to send acceptances or regrets. Most likely, yes. My aunt seldom refuses an invitation."

As Sarah launched into a list of those likely to attend, Felicity listened halfheartedly until a certain name was mentioned.

". . . and Viscount Pentclair has accepted, I hear. Is he not a handsome rake? Although I vow, Sir Justin is much too serious for my taste. I prefer a man with a happier disposition. Such as your brother. Did I tell you . . ."

But now Felicity was not listening at all. So Justin would be here in two weeks. She knew she could not bear the pain of seeing him again, nor even of being in the same house with him. She must remember to develop a crushing headache at the appropriate time.

". . . and there," Sarah was saying, "Lady Ashford stood, ankle-deep in a puddle, with her slippers dissolving in the mud!"

"Indeed?" Felicity murmured. "Do tell."

"Yer lordship?" Mick called out over the paddock. "Gentleman to see you."

Augustus frowned at the head groom, then turned with an affectionate grin back to Emperor. He fed the stallion the rest of the apple, brushed the animal's silky forelock regretfully, and with a sigh went off to see who was bothering him now.

"Henning!" he said with some cheer, seeing his neighbor. "Come on out to the paddock. I want to show you—"

"If you do not mind, Sir Augustus," Edmund said with a nervous smile, "I should like a word with you."

"Well, speak up, man," Augustus encouraged him with good nature.

Dubiously Edmund glanced about. "I believe that what I have to say requires a more private, perhaps a more formal setting."

Augustus sighed. "If you insist. Come up to the house."

They passed Harriet, who was seated on a bench on the terrace, devouring the latest gossip sheet from London.

"This would be suitable," Henning said suddenly. "In

point of fact, I should like Lady Harriet to join us, if she pleases."

Harriet glanced up from her reading. "Certainly, Sir Edmund. Please do sit. May I offer you a glass of iced lemonade?"

"Thank you, no. And I should prefer to stand, if you do not mind."

Harriet shrugged. "Suit yourself. Brother-in-law?"

Augustus leaned back, resting against the thick stone half-wall that surrounded the terrace, glancing wistfully down toward the stables. "None for me, thank you."

Clearing his throat, Henning finally said, "I have come on a matter of some importance, and since I am not proficient in chitchat, I shall get straight to the point."

"Always a sound idea," Harriet said with vast approval, folding her paper reluctantly.

"I wish," Edmund said formally, "to offer for Lady Felicity."

The Bellwoods gaped at him.

"You do?" Harriet managed weakly at last. "What a surprise."

Augustus was not so polite. "By dam . . . er, Jupiter, man, you are of the same age as I."

"Not quite," Edmund dissented. "I am six-and-thirty, and in excellent health. I could provide a comfortable and happy life for your daughter."

"Er, Sir Edmund," Harriet put in hesitantly, "I do not seem to recall Felicity mentioning anything concerning . . ."

"I have not spoken with her yet, madam. Considering her obvious inexperience in these matters, I thought I should speak first with you.

"But let me reassure you," he continued, addressing them both, "that I have spoken with her of other matters and have discovered that we have remarkably similar tastes. She apparently loves the country, having little use for London, as do I. I believe she is fond of riding. I, too, enjoy a leisurely jaunt about the fields. All in all, she seems a shy, quiet miss with a temperament that suits my own.''

"Felicity?" Harriet blurted with an incredulous gaze. Recovering, she hastened to repair the damage. "Well, yes, of course. She is a well-bred young lady.''

Henning nodded in agreement. "I believe we should get on quite well together.''

Augustus glared at his sister-in-law with a look that accused her of being responsible for this state of affairs. Throwing the glare back at him, Harriet did not speak for a moment. Then she faced Henning with a slight smile.

"We are deeply honored by your offer, Sir Edmund,'' she said smoothly. "But at the moment, Felicity is considering the offers of two other gentlemen who have beaten you to the gate. I shall certainly inform her of your very great compliment to her, and I know she will also consider your offer seriously.''

Henning regarded her for a moment, then smiled slightly. "Perhaps this may be callous of me, but since we may soon be related by marriage . . . Do you know my great-uncle William?''

Harriet raised her eyebrows. "The Duke of Wilshire? I believe I might have made his acquaintance at one time. An elderly gentleman, is he not? I certainly know *of* him.''

"Perhaps you did not realize that he is in poor health. He is not expected to live out the year.''

"Oh, I am sorry,'' Harriet said reflexively, her polite expression not having altered a whit.

"And perhaps you also did not know,'' Henning continued evenly, "that his only son, my cousin Richard, recently was felled by a virulent fever while traveling in Greece and died en route back to England. Richard was a bachelor.''

He paused to allow the full effect of his revelation to penetrate. "It appears that I am my great-uncle's heir."

"You are . . ." Harriet's mouth dropped open. "The title comes to you?"

"Not until Great-Uncle William expires," Edmund said bluntly. "Perhaps now you see my concern. My first wife and I were not blessed with children. And so, besides having the tenderest and most honorable affection for Lady Felicity, I also shall soon be duty-bound to produce the next heir to the dukedom. I very much should like Lady Felicity to be my duchess."

"Duchess!" Harriet breathed, her eyes shining. "Oh, Sir Edmund. You have touched my heart with your sincere fondness for Felicity. And I am certain that you will touch hers also."

"Then," Henning said, his face flushing eagerly, "I may speak with her?"

"Why, certainly, Sir Edmund!"

Henning turned to Augustus. "You concur?"

Augustus frowned. "We shall see what Lissie has to say."

"Which," Harriet added, shooting him a warning glance, "is sure to be in Sir Edmund's favor."

At that, Edmund asked, "Is she free at the moment? May I speak with her now?"

"Well, not just now," Harriet said hastily. She hesitated, thinking swiftly. "May I be candid with you, Sir Edmund? You were correct in your judgment that she is inexperienced in these matters. I believe that she might be so stunned if you should spring this upon her unprepared, she might succumb to a case of the vapors. I fear such an event might upset you dreadfully. Am I correct?"

"Dreadfully," Edmund agreed with obvious concern.

"Then may I suggest," Harriet went on silkily, "that you permit me to speak with her first. To prepare her gently, so that your offer may not come as such a surprise to her.''

"That seems a splendid plan," Henning said with much relief. "When might I call on Lady Felicity?"

"This is a delicate matter," Harriet said slowly, thinking. "I should like to prepare her gradually. Perhaps a day or two . . . Yes. Dine with us on the day after tomorrow. After dinner, you may speak to Felicity."

Henning beamed. "Splendid! I deeply appreciate your aid in this matter."

"It will be my pleasure, Sir Edmund," Harriet cooed.

Henning turned to Augustus and pumped his hand enthusiastically. "Sir. Thank you. I will provide your daughter with everything she ever could desire."

"How's the state of your library?" Augustus growled abruptly.

"I beg your pardon?"

Harriet jumped up and stepped between the men, gently steering Henning away before Augustus would spoil the match of a lifetime.

"Sir Edmund. Until we see you in two days, then? *Au revoir*."

"Good day, madam. Sir Augustus."

He departed with what Harriet would vow was a bouyancy in his step. When he was far out of earshot, she turned to her brother-in-law triumphantly.

"A duchess!" she cried, clasping her hands together ecstatically. "What do you think of my matchmaking now, Augustus?"

"Let us see," he repeated stubbornly, "what Lissie has to say."

Harriet waved a disparaging hand. "Oh, bother. When I explain it all to her, when I point out the incredible advantages of this match, she will accept his offer so swiftly, the duke's head will spin."

"Henning's not a duke yet," Augustus pointed out nastily. "At least allow old William a few last breaths before you bury him."

"Now, or next year," Harriet replied in an airy tone, "what difference does it make? Our own Felicity is marrying a duke!"

"Let us see," Augustus said one final time, "what Lissie has to say."

18

"Felicity? Am I disturbing you, dear?"

Felicity looked up from her writing table. "No, Aunt Harriet. Do come in."

Harriet casually approached her, glancing at Felicity's poised quill. "Oh, I am interrupting you."

"Not at all," Felicity protested, blotting the paper upon which she had been writing. "I have just finished a note to Sarah Sumner. She is a pleasant miss, do you not agree?"

"Yes, a sweet little article," Harriet commented idly, toying with a quill wiper. "Where is Milly?"

"She took my things to the laundry maid."

Felicity looked at her aunt a bit askance. Harriet so seldom came unsolicited to Felicity's room.

"If you are wondering, Milly is performing quite well as my abigail. Although I shall never hear the last of Nanny's moanings about being set out to pasture. You were entirely correct, Aunt Harriet. Poor Nanny's fingers are so bent, she cannot manage even the largest of buttons. But in truth, while she grumbles she enjoys her freer time."

"Good, I am happy to hear that." Suddenly Harriet added, "Felicity, come sit with me."

She pulled Felicity over to the chaise longue, which was

182

conveniently situated to catch the afternoon breeze. When they were settled, she grasped Felicity's hands lightly in her own.

"My dear, a most important event is upcoming on Friday."

"Yes, I know," Felicity said quickly, and launched into her rehearsed speech. "Lady Ashford's house party. Oh, aunt, I dread telling you this, but I have been developing a vague malaise all day. Nothing serious, mind you. My head is achy, and I feel generally depleted. I think perhaps I have overtired myself."

Anxiously her aunt pressed a hand to Felicity's brow. "You are not feverish, are you? No, thank the heavens, your forehead is cool. Quickly, we must get you into bed—"

"No, no," Felicity protested mildly. "I am certain that my condition will improve markedly with a few days' respite from social activities. I merely need a bit of idle time to catch up my correspondence, or to read the book of poetry Lady Ashford presented to me, perhaps."

"Send Milly to me for my headache powders," Harriet ordered. "With a strong cup of tea, they work wonders. You will be set to rights in a day."

Felicity sighed. "I am certain I shall. But I still doubt that I could withstand the rigors of a house party, with one activity after another. I fear you must tender my regrets to Lady Ashford."

With a smug smile, Harriet said, "I have sent the note off ten minutes ago."

Felicity blinked, surprised by her easy, even premature victory. "You have?"

"Yes, indeed. And for the most marvelous reason in the world."

Carefully Felicity asked, "And what might that be?"

"We," Harriet announced, savoring her very words, "are entertaining a duke!"

"Oh, yes?" Felicity said politely. Whatever plot Harriet had in mind could not cause her half the trepidation that the prospect of encountering Justin at Ashford Hall did.

"Well, he may not be a duke when we dine on Friday, but in no longer than a few months he will be." She leaned forward, her eyes gleaming. "And this is the most delicious news of all. Felicity, what do you think? The man has offered for you!"

Felicity stared at her, bewildered. "He . . . But who is this man?"

"Before I reveal his identity," Harriet said craftily, "allow me to to tell you a bit about him. He is a fine-looking gentleman, and possesses an even temperament. I cannot imagine him ever raising his voice, nor speaking cruelly, nor falling prey to even the mildest of melancholia. He is strong enough to be dependable, but with no proclivity toward harshness or tyranny. He is deligent in his duties, has absolutely no vices whatever, and descends from an excellent family."

Harriet laughed gaily. "Well, naturally, an excellent family. He is a duke, after all!"

Felicity did not know what to say, but the longer her aunt spoke, the more uneasy she became.

"And," Harriet confided excitedly, "you will be pleased to know that you and he share many interests in common. He much prefers bucolic country life to the pace of town. He rides for hours daily, and is sure to have a prime stable. Oh, my dear, the two of you are a perfect match!"

Definitely unnerved now, Felicity asked quietly, "Who is he, aunt?"

With a smile that seemed suspiciously bright to Felicity, Harriet said, "Prepare yourself for a lovely surprise, my dear. He is, or is about to be, the Duke of Wilshire. Sir Edmund Henning!''

Gasping, Felicity stared at her. ''Our neighbor, Sir Edmund? But, Aunt Harriet, surely you jest with me. Sir Edmund has offered for me?''

''Yes, indeed. Is that not simply marvelous?''

''But . . . but . . .'' Felicity sputtered, scarcely crediting what she had just heard. ''He is of my father's age.''

''Not quite,'' Harriet corrected blandly, ''but what an advantage that is.''

''Advantage? *Advantage*?''

''But of course. He is long done with the impetuosity of youth. He will never vex you by staying out all hours gaming and drinking. And even better, he has had prior matrimonial experience with his first wife, God rest her soul. Being wedded will prove an easy adjustment for him. And trust my wisdom in this, my dear: a gentleman of a certain age who marries a younger woman will always treat her regally. He considers her a precious prize—''

''Oh, yes?'' Felicity blurted sardonically. ''Will he present me with a blue ribbon to wear, like a champion Jersey cow on Fair Day?''

Harriet patted her hand in gentle reproach. ''Now, Felicity, do not be vulgar. Think in practical terms for a moment. You decidedly hold the winning hand in this game.''

''Not if I choose not to play,'' Felicity retorted, her blue eyes sparking. ''Oh, Aunt Harriet, really! I could no sooner wed Sir Edmund than . . . than . . . Mick McCafferty!''

Closing her eyes, Harriet said, ''How could you mention the Duke of Wilshire and our head groom in the same breath?''

''Because,'' Felicity said tartly, ''to my mind, the absurdity of marrying either of them is the same. In truth, were I pressed, I should prefer Mick!''

Harriet glared at her. "That will be quite enough, Felicity. Your father and I have given Sir Edmund cause to believe you will look upon his suit with favor."

"Papa is part of this scheme?" Felicity asked softly, her eyes taking on an injured cast.

"Felicity, when will you realize that your father and I, having had much more experience in this world than you, may understand what is best for you when you do not?"

Felicity gazed bleakly at her aunt. Her despair could find no words.

With a deep sigh, Harriet peered bluntly at her niece.

"My dear, you must face the reality of your situation. Whether the notion pleases you or causes you the greatest of displeasure, you will be wedded to some man. That is an immutable fact. So you may as well make a silk purse from what to you, obviously, is a sow's ear. Why not accept a man who is prepared to give you the finest the world can offer?"

Helpless tears formed in Felicity's eyes, and she clutched her aunt's arm in supplication. "Aunt Harriet, I implore you. Do not force me to go through with this. Allow me to remain here, caring for Papa—"

"We have been over this ground before," Harriet reminded her, gently disengaging her hand. "It is your father's wish that you marry. You will break his heart, perhaps even hasten his death, if he is forced to worry day by day about your fate. Your father is not a young man, Felicity. Do you wish to send him to an early grave over his concern for you?"

"No," she whispered, bowing her head, the tears spilling down her cheeks.

"Naturally you do not. Now, view the subject of Sir Edmund from this perspective: once you are wedded, once his great-uncle passes from this earth, you will be a duchess." Harriet paused a moment. "I hesitate to tell you this, for fear of encouraging what I have always suspected as a streak of eccentricity in you. But as we are speaking of practicalities, I must mention this in all fairness.''

Harriet gazed speculatively at her niece. ''Do you have any notion of the power a duchess possesses? She is less bound by rules of convention than any of her lessers. I have seen a lady of that rank wear a shawl that looked as if it had come off her horse's back, and no one batted an eye. Indeed, the next day, every modiste in London was plied with orders for the same fabric. I once attended a soiree where a certain dowager duchess insisted that her pug dog be served at table, and the hostess graciously piled cushions on the chair so that the animal might lap at its plate. Again, conversation flowed naturally through the dining salon as if nothing out of the ordinary were occurring right before our very eyes. Oh, certainly, ladies of such eccentric tastes may rate a few lines in the scandal sheets. But such a mention simply makes them more desirable guests at the next affair.''

Harriet reached out to tilt up Felicity's chin and gazed into Felicity's tearful eyes. ''Do you not see the power you will achieve, to determine in large measure the course of your own days? By virtue of your beauty and your title, the *ton* will excuse behavior they might find intolerable in one below your rank. Once you are wedded, my dear, you will be afforded much of the liberty to choose your own fate that you so desire. You may bury your nose in books all the day long, even be recognized as a legitimate bluestocking, with no damage to your reputation. You will be considered somewhat of an unorthodox duchess, to be sure. But that label will merely serve to pique the curiosity of the *haunt monde*.''

With a slight smile, Harriet patted her niece's hand. ''All that is required is an amiable husband, and I am convinced that Sir Edmund will be such a man. He is completely besotted with you, my dear. He actually has declared before your father and me that he will provide you with your heart's desire. Believe me, Felicity, you could not find a more perfect mate for yourself if you searched for a thousand years.''

By now, Felicity's head ached in earnest. She pressed her fingers to her temples.

"Oh, Aunt Harriet, I feel such confusion."

"Certainly you do, my dear," Harriet replied cheerily. "I have given you much food for thought. But do consider my words, Felicity. I think you will realize that Sir Edmund affords you the greatest chance of happiness."

Reluctantly Felicity nodded. "I will consider what you have told me."

With a relieved sigh that seemed to come from her heart, Harriet said, "Splendid! Now. Where can Milly be? Never mind, I shall send Grendall in with hte headache powders and a pot of strong tea. You rest now, my dear. I shall have a tray sent up for your supper. And I shall insist that Cook include upon it one of your favorite pear tarts. Even two of them! This is no time to worry about your figure."

She rose and turned to depart. At the doorway, she said firmly, "If you need me for any reason, if you simply wish to chat, send for me immediately. I shall be at your beck and call. Good day, my dear."

With a brief wave, Harriet was gone.

Incredibly weary, Felicity reclined on the chaise longue. She closed her eyes and rubbed at her temples until Milly returned a few minutes later and began putting away the freshly laundered garments she had brought.

"Oh, milady," the newly appointed abigail moaned. "That Rosie! Her wits are right addled, and make no mistake. Lost yer blue lace gloves, she did, and didn't we search through six baskets o' laundry afore we found 'em . . . Milady, are you ailin? You look a mite peaked."

"Grendall is bringing me powders and tea," Felicity murmured. "Would you help me into my dressing gown?"

Later, having ingested the headache remedy with half the pot of tea and dismissing Milly, Felicity lay back once again on the chaise longue. Released from her confining day dress, with her hair loosened and spilling around her shoulders, she did feel marginally better. But so many weeks had passed since she had set her wits to any problem more exacting than which gown to choose, Felicity was slow to organize her thoughts.

Although her first instinct was to rebel against the entire proposal, she knew she must own to recognizing the merit in Harriet's words. Perhaps Edmund Henning was indeed her means to a life more suited to her nature. She had never considered that the key to her freedom might lie in marrying the properly amenable man. . . .

But that thought was a lie, Felicity reminded herself sadly. The man she first had asked to be her liberator was Justin. Swiftly she drew a veil over her thoughts of him.

With a great sense of exhaustion, she realized that in a few short months she had gone from a determination never to marry anyone, to a wrenching and fruitless desire to wed a man she loved desperately, to an unemotional deliberation regarding a match with a man she scarcely knew.

Henning was not a disagreeable sort, she told herself now. A bit dull, perhaps even boring, he nonetheless seemed to be the sort of man that she could control with relative ease.

Listening to her own reasoning, Felicity recoiled with distaste at her cold assessment of a man who would be her life's mate. But pragmatic assessment was exactly what her situation required. In actuality, she might rather enjoy the life of an eccentric duchess. She would be granted her most fervent wish: to say and to do precisely what she chose, with no one to force her to build walls between whom they wished to see and who she truly was.

Why, she would fare far better as a duly wedded duchess than as an unmarried, closely watched girl. Yes, indeed, she told herself, Henning's offer for her was a stroke of luck that she could ill afford to pass up.

Suddenly Felicity burst into tears, and for a solid fifteen minutes she sobbed and beat her fist into the pillow. Then, gradually purged, she trailed off into sniffling silence and drifted into a sleep of exhaustion.

Sometime later she awoke to discover that a strange sense of calm had descended upon her. Felicity bathed her face in the cool water of the basin, rang for Milly, and dressed in a white gown dotted with yellow rosebuds. She went down to the dining salon and joined Harriet and Augustus just as they were sitting down to dinner.

"Felicity," Harriet said in surprise, "have you recovered from your headache, dear?"

"Yes, I have," Felicity said, sitting in the chair that the footman held for her. "The remedies you sent me worked wonders."

"Oh, I am so relieved. Did you consider what I told you?"

Felicity looked at her aunt with a clear gaze. "Yes. And I saw the sensibility of your words. I have decided to accept Sir Edmund's offer."

Harriet beamed with happiness, and also, it was obvious, vast relief. "This announcement warrants a toast."

She raised her wineglass and gestured for Augustus to do the same.

"To Felicity," she intoned with satisfaction. "The next Duchess of Wilshire!"

Augustus drank, reluctantly it seemed, then peered at his daughter. "Are you certain, Lissie?"

Felicity put on a bright smile and replied, "Yes, Papa."

"I must talk with Dobbs after dinner," Harriet said excitedly. "The meal on Friday must be absolutely perfect. Oh, and I must send for Georgina straightaway. And little do I care if the entire Exchequer goes into dun territory. Hubert must come too. And Peter. Oh, dear, I do hope Peter can manage to behave himself for one evening."

"Invite Lady Sarah," Felicity suggested calmly, placing her serviette on her lap. "Peter will behave impeccably."

"Marvelous idea!" Harriet crowed. "Who knows? Perhaps the spirit of the evening will inspire your brother. Perhaps he will on the very same night offer for Sarah. Would that not be a happy turn of events?"

"Who is Sarah?" Augustus muttered, perplexed.

"Well, brother-in-law," Harriet answered tartly, "if you should poke your head out from the stables occasionally, you might notice that your son has developed a *tendre* for a certain Lady Sarah Sumner, daughter of Lord Wentham. She is a comely miss, and Peter seems quite taken with her."

"High time that boy settles himself," Augustus proclaimed stoutly. "Good to hear he is feeling his oats and sniffing around a filly."

"Really, Augustus," Harriet said disapprovingly. Then her brow wrinkled in concern. "I do hope you will remember to restrain yourself from such vulgarities while the duke-to-be is present on Friday. I do hope you will show the proper respect."

Augustus snorted. "Madam, I have been acquainted with Edmund Henning for twenty years. I am not about to change my attitude toward him now."

"What! Do you intend to ruin Felicity's good fortune even before it comes to pass? Are you mad?"

"Certainly not. I simply have no intention to mewling about like a sick cat. If I cannot speak my mind in my own house, madam . . ."

   While her father and her aunt waged their battle, Felicity
closed off her ears and calmly began eating her consommé.
She concentrated on the act of bringing the broth to her mouth
and tried to erase all her thoughts.

   But one phrase kept echoing in her mind. Her father's first
question to her.

   "Are you certain, Lissie?"

   She heard his voice repeated over and over in her mind.
But for the life of her, she could not hear her own answer.

19

From the very moment of dawn on Friday morning, the heat began building. By noon the sun blazed down from a sky bleached nearly white from intensity. And nightfall brought little relief, with the heat having baked into the fields and stone buildings all the day long.

Harriet hastily arranged to have twenty of the footmen to ring the dining salon, waving long-handled fans to circulate the stagnant air. She intended, she told Felicity firmly, to let nothing, not even an uncooperative Nature, ruin her entertainment of the next Duke of Wilshire.

Sir Edmund arrived promptly at half-past eight, greeting Felicity with a nervous but pleasant smile and a large bouquet of pink and white roses. The rest of the dinner party were already assembled in the drawing room. Augustus played the role of genial host, with nary an oath or vulgarity passing his lips. Harriet chatted charmingly with all and sundry, paying especial attention, of course, to the guest of honor. Peter and Sarah grinned at each other continually, even while conversing with the others. Even Georgina and Hubert joined in the generally jolly mood, although Felicity thought she detected a layer of unhappiness under their smiles.

At nine, they repaired to the dining salon. Harriet had

ordered a meal to outshine any of her previous efforts. Every
delicacy imaginable found its way to the Bellwood table that
evening: from the first offering of lobster patties in a creamy
sauce, through nine courses, and ending with a flambé of
pineapple and cherries. Felicity knew to eat but a few morsels
of each dish, and still, by midnight, when the last course
was cleared and they rose from the table, she was completely
sated.

"On such a fine evening, Sir Edmund," she heard Aunt
Harriet saying casually, "perhaps you would prefer to forgo
the gentleman's cigars and port and take a stroll on the
terrace. I am certain that Felicity would be delighted to show
you around."

Henning gulped and nodded, looking expectantly at
Felicity. Inhaling deeply, she pasted on a smile and took his
arm.

They slowly made a turn from one end of the long terrace
to the other in silence. Finally Edmund stopped and placed
his kerchief on the stone bench for her. Obligingly she sat,
while he remained standing beside her. The moonlight, along
with the torches set at intervals on the terrace, illuminated
them both clearly.

"Warm evening," Edmund commented unnecessarily,
wiping his brow. Felicity allowed that it was.

"Lady Felicity," he finally blurted, "I have neither the
temperament nor the time to approach important matters in
a flowery fashion. I take it that your aunt has spoken to you
about my offer?"

"Yes, she has."

"Well, then, Lady Felicity. I can give you all the wordly
goods you might ever in good taste desire, as well as the
eventual rank of duchess. So in light of my deepest affection
and greatest respect for you, would you consent to be my
wife?"

Felicity blinked at him. Certainly she had not expected declarations of undying love from him, but neither had she foreseen such a wooden demeanor in his proposal.

"Well, Lady Felicity?"

His impatience annoyed her. Even if he did perceive offering marriage to her as a business dealing, he might have approached her in a more gentle manner.

She smiled tightly. "Tell me, Sir Edmund. As my husband, what might you expect of me?"

Henning frowned, obviously not prepared for the idea that he might need to persuade her.

"Well, er, that you always remain the sweet, shy woman you are. I cannot abide loud, opinionated women. My late wife was of that breed. One of your most prominent attractions is that you have very little to say."

"Why, thank you," Felicity murmured dryly.

"And," he continued, "I would expect you to keep the nursery filled with children. I should like seven or eight, I believe. To ensure the title. That would be your primary duty."

"Of course," Felicity said sweetly.

"And . . . oh, I cannot think of anything other than that. Except, naturally, that you always represent me in the most impeccable fashion. Which," he hastily added, "I know you will. I cannot imagine a breath of scandal ever approaching you."

Felicity looked at Edmund, so straight and serious in his stance, with perspiration gleaming on his florid face and dripping into his cravat.

"Tell me, Sir Edmund," she said softly, "about the state of your library."

"My library? I have no idea. I never enter the room. And of course, you would not be expected to either. So you may dismiss your qualms on that account." He rubbed his hands together briskly. "Now. Since I have answered your queries, will you answer mine? Will you consent to be my wife?"

Felicity pondered for a moment, but not over the question Edmund had asked. She saw now that despite Harriet's sincerely related perception of the life of a duchess, the conclusion her aunt had made was false. There could be no freedom for Felicity in any sort of servitude to a man. Either she would be accepted for her true temperament or she would live forever unwedded, regardless of what anyone in her family thought. Aunt Harriet might rant and rave, but her father would never turn her out of the house, and she could cope with Harriet's disapproval.

Finally she rose, and for the first time since she could remember, her smile was genuine.

"Sir Edmund, I shall be happy to tell you my answer. But first, allow me a few words. You are a kind man, I am certain, and a dutiful one. The mantle of Duke of Wilshire will rest splendidly upon your shoulders. And many young ladies would be proud and thrilled and perfectly suited to be your duchess."

Felicity sighed. "Unfortunately, I am not one of them. I am just what you most dread, a loud, opinionated woman. I have certain preferences that would cause you to turn positively green from distaste. I read incessantly, everything from Homer's accounts of the Trojan Wars to Pythagoras and the theory of mathematics. I neither notice nor care if the dust is an inch thick on the mantelpiece. I even, on a few occasions, have ridden my horse astride."

Edmund gasped in horror, staring at her as if she had just grown a set of horns.

"So you can see, Sir Edmund," Felicity said cheerfully, "that I would make you a dismal wife. Thank you for the very great honor of asking me, but be grateful that I cannot accept."

"I . . . I . . ." Edmund sputtered, his chest heaving and actually popping a stud from his shirt. "This is outrageous! That your aunt tried to pass you off as quality goods when you are naught but a fast piece of baggage!"

Felicity took a step nearer to him, and Edmund cringed. "I am nothing of the sort," she said quietly, fixing him with an unwavering stare. "And if you say so again, I shall punch you in the eye. I am an intelligent woman of eccentric taste, and if you cannot accept my nature, it is to your discredit, not mine. Good evening, Sir Edmund."

Leaving him gawking in openmouthed terror, Felicity turned and left. But she did not return to the house. She gathered up the skirts of her cream-colored gown and began to run. The pinnings came loose from her chignon, and her auburn tresses flowed freely down her back. Over the lawn of clipped grass and down the gravel path toward the stables she flew, ripping to shreds the silk slippers meant for nothing more strenuous than gliding across a ballroom floor.

Glimpsing a light shining from the tack room, she hurried inside. Mick and a few of the grooms were seated on the floor with bottles of stout, rolling a pair of dice.

"Milady!" the head groom gasped, and they all froze in apprehension.

"Good evening, Mick, lads," Felicity sang out. "Who is winning?"

"Er, I am," Mick said reluctantly. "Milady, what are you doing here?"

"I am going for a ride. Would you mind preparing Sheba for me?"

"A ride? At this hour? Beggin' yer pardon, milady, but have you gone mad?"

Felicity laughed. "No. In point of fact, I have just found my wits. Oh, and do not put the lady's version on her, Mick. I want a gentleman's saddle." Glancing at her gown, she

added, "Do you suppose you might find a suit of clothes
for me? The tiger who rode Emperor in the race is of the
same stature as I."

After numerous protests that her father would skin him
alive, and Felicity's cheerful assurances that without his help
she would manage alone, Mick finally relented. As one of
the other grooms saddled Sheba, he brought clean clothing
for her, the same outfitting that the tiger had worn in the race.

The grooms quickly cleared out of the tack room, and
Felicity, faced with the dilemma of a long row of buttons
down the back of her gown, finally shrugged and ripped the
fine lawn fabric from neck to waist. She dressed in the buff-
colored breeches and dark red brass-buttoned coat, pleased
that the clothing fitted her passably well. The tall black boots
were too large, but she solved that problem by stuffing wads
of batiste ripped from her gown into the toes. Finally she
wound her hair in a knot and pulled a jockey cap down on
her head to hold it in place.

Sheba whinnied in pleasure to see her. With a boost from
Mick, she was on the mare's back.

"At least," Mick pleaded with her, "let me send one o'
the lads with ye, milady. 'Tis not fittin' to go abroad alone
at this hour."

"He will never keep up with me, Mick. Besides, I can
outrun anyone who might wish me harm. Good-bye!"

A high full moon had rendered the darkness as clear as
day. Felicity knew she could cut the time of her journey by
two-thirds merely by riding over the meadows and pastures
in the stead of keeping to the post road. With a determined
smile, she tapped Sheba lightly with the crop and set off in
the direction of Ashford Hall.

Lights blazed throughout the great house. The sound of
musicians playing a lively country dance greeted Felicity as

she halted Sheba at the entrance. She handed over the reins to a liveried footman, who did not so much as blink at her unusual costume. As Felicity bounded up the stairs and into the entry hall, she noticed a dashing cavalier flirting with a dairymaid. The sight took her aback until she realized it was the night of Lady Ashford's masquerade ball.

"Oho!" the cavalier shouted drunkenly, seeing her and edging closer. "And what have we here? A tiger, no doubt. And by the delicacy of that retroussé nose and the charming fringe around those lovely blue eyes, I should say 'tis a female of the species, at that. Where is your mask, Madam Jockey?"

In answer, Felicity pulled the lace kerchief from his sleeve and tied it across her face so that only her eyes showed. He laughed in appreciation of her gesture, and Felicity brushed past him and hurried to the ballroom.

Every period from early Egypt to present-day Russia, and historical personages from Good Queen Bess to Ghengis Khan, were represented in the costumes. After only a few moments, she spotted Justin standing alone off to the side.

She recognized him in spite of his costume disguise and half-mask. He was dressed as a buccaneer, in a full opened-necked shirt and black breeches, with a gold hoop in his ear. Her pulse leapt wildly and she inhaled gulps of air until her heart settled to a quieter beat. Then, determinedly, Felicity weaved her way through the revelers until she stood before him.

He looked the horse jockey up and down with an amused grin. But when their gazes met, his smile froze in recognition.

"Good evening, Justin," she said, the silk kerchief muffling the slight tremor in her voice. "I should like to speak with you, and since you most likely will not want anyone to overhear what I have to say, I suggest we go somewhere more private."

Without a word, he took her elbow and guided her to the farthest end of the house, tossing away his mask and picking up two lighted candelabra from the hallway as he went. He led her to a small anteroom off the conservatory, where Lady Ashford's flowers were trimmed and arranged daily. Setting the candelabra down on the worktable, he crossed his arms and stared at her.

"Well?" he demanded boldly.

20

Slowly Felicity untied the kerchief from around her face, took off her cap, and shook out her hair. She noticed the subsequent flicker in Justin's eye.

"I am done with masquerades," she said quietly, with more confidence than she felt. "I want to know the entire truth."

He leaned toward her and Felicity detected the strong scent of brandy on his breath. It did not matter to her. Perhaps the spirit would loosen his tongue to honest explanations.

"About my true identity as a highwayman? About my stealing jewels? I have told you the truth." His eyes gleamed. "I hope you appreciate the irony of my costume. This pirate does not plunder on the bounding main, but in the finest houses of England."

"So you have said. What I want to know is why. And none of your intellectual diversions, falsehoods every one."

With a bitter grin he said, "I am what I am, madam. You may accept it or not, it makes no difference to me."

"Rubbish!" Felicity retorted furiously. "I know you, Justin, and you are not a callous thief."

Her voice faltered, but she plunged ahead, having come too far to back away now.

"I know you," she repeated softly, gazing at him and feeling her love for him bursting through the walls, overwhelmingly strong and radiant. "I have spent the last half-hour thinking back over every moment I have spent with you, realizing that I saw your true colors long ago. They are the colors of honor, and compassion, and goodness. But for some reason, you have chosen to hide your real self behind a wall and show me the face of a jewel thief. I am well-versed in the properties of walls, Justin, and permit me to say that they are double-edged conveniences. They prevent the world from seeing who you are, but they also prevent you from being true to yourself. Soon you begin to believe you are that false mask you allow the world to see. And behind the walls, your true feelings roil and churn, and succeed either in throwing you into madness or in destroying you."

She stepped toward him, peering at him earnestly. "There is no danger in revealing who you truly are. Only in insisting upon pretending to be who you are not."

Justin smiled tightly, his dark eyes gleaming. "You do not want to know. Trust me in this, Felicity. The truth will shatter your innocent little world and you will never recover from it."

"I can bear anything you have to say to me," she insisted hotly, "except another of your pretenses. Tell me!"

"No. Leave it." Angry bolts shot from his gaze.

She beat her fist against the solid mass of his broad chest. "Tell me!" she cried.

Suddenly Justin grasped her arms, his face inches from hers. "Tell you? Very well, I will! Brace yourself, Felicity, because it is an ugly tale."

Leaning back, he gazed at her, that strange and rather frightening glint in his eyes glowing brighter. "I am the dupe of the treachery of women. My late wife, Alice, to be precise. Like you, Felicity, she was a strong-willed thing, obsessed with doing exactly as she pleased. And what pleased her most was her . . . dalliances with other men.

"Do you take my meaning, Felicity?" he asked, his voice soft but fearfully intense. "Can you understand the extent of her ruthless quest to be daring? Alice was democratic at her play. She would choose peers of the realm or stableboys. My friends were her special favorite, though. She took inordinate pleasure in seducing my friends."

Justin gritted his teeth, but continued in that same dangerously quiet and bitter tone. "And Alice had one more endearing little quirk. She would accept no tokens of affection from her paramours. Oh, no. She insisted upon giving *them* the tokens. And do you know what she chose for her generous gifts to her lovers? The Havilland family jewels!"

Felicity could see that the very idea so enraged him, he had to stop to regain a semblance of composure. She was, indeed, completely horrified, but she knew she could not express the slightest reaction, if he were to spill out the entire story. She longed to mitigate his anger and obvious pain, but she was numb with shock and could not utter a word.

"And so, my inquisitive Felicity," Justin growled, "you now understand why I became a jewel thief. My family honor demanded no less. My personal honor was destroyed long ago. I merely did not know it. Alice went on for years, while I was away at the wars, and while I was living in the same home. Fool that I was, I never suspected." He laughed harshly. "Would you like to know how I found out? Alice had a slight mishap. She chose as one of her conquests an older gentleman with a weak heart. He expired in our very home. She could not very well hide that from me. And so when I called her the name for what she was, the entire story came tumbling out. Oh, did I mention the identity of that older gentleman? He was one of my father's friends: your uncle, Octavius Bellwood."

Inwardly Felicity groaned. Her own uncle.

"I managed to get Octavius back to his own town house. I concocted some Banbury tale for Harriet, but I have always suspected that she knew the truth. When I returned home, Alice had gone. I never saw her again. Bold wench that she was, she wrote to me from across the Continent, asking me to send her funds. I gladly did so, simply to keep her out of my sight. Eventually I learned that she had drowned in a storm off the Dalmatian coast."

He looked at Felicity with a sour, ironic gaze. "I had her body shipped back to England, just to assure myself that she truly was dead and gone from my life. What do you think of me now, Miss Seeker of Truth?"

The glint in his eyes had changed. What Felicity saw now was a man hoping against hope for a lifeline to pull him out of the fire of his own personal hell. She swallowed hard, realizing that the next words she spoke might be the most vital she would ever speak in her life.

"I think," she said softly, her voice trembling not with fear but with compassion, "that you have been wounded beyond measure. That you have only done what you thought would best repair the damage to your honor. That you have walled up your pain and your anger, and that by containing them so deeply inside with no outlet, you have forced them to attempt to destroy you from within.

"And I think," she continued steadily, "that I have never loved you so much as I do at this very moment."

Justin's mask of anger crumpled and his eyes filled with the purest anguish Felicity could imagine. With a moan deep in his throat, he reached for her, crushing her to his chest.

"Oh, my dearest," he whispered passionately, "God help me, but I love you too. And that is why I must let you go."

"No," she cried, pressing her lips to the smooth flesh of his neck.

"Oh, yes." He held her tight in his embrace, his hand caressing her hair. "I am not fit for a strong-minded woman now. I would need to control you in order to feel secure in my love for you. And that would destroy you, Felicity, my dearest. You are a true free spirit, and any attempts to shackle you would cause you to despise me eventually. And that would destroy me."

Gently he relaxed his embrace and looked down at her eyes. "You are the soul of goodness and beauty," he murmured, his belief in his words reflected in his lambent gaze. "And I shall love you forever."

With that, his lips descended upon hers, and in the tender strength of his kiss, Felicity tasted bittersweet love and longing.

Suddenly he pulled her arms from around him.

"I am leaving tonight," he said softly. "I have booked passage to Venice. For a while, at least, I think I could not bear to be in the same country as you, knowing I cannot have you. Good-bye, Felicity. My love."

He wheeled and bolted through the conservatory and out into the night.

"Justin, no!" she cried, running after him. "Wait! Wait!" But he was gone.

Felicity sat listlessly upon her mare, her head aching, her thoughts tangled. She had no energy for any pace faster than a walk, although Sheba whinnied impatiently to set off over the fields.

Her heart swung from elation that Justin loved her to despair that he had left her. For an hour after he had disappeared from the conservatory, she had searched the grounds almost frantically. But when she finally had inquired of the grooms, she had discovered that he indeed had claimed his horse. And naturally they had no idea in which direction he had ridden.

Finding him would do no good at any rate, sh realized. He had spoken from his true feelings when he said he feared their mutual destruction. And perhaps he was even correct, Felicity thought sadly. Perhaps too much of the past would forever discolor their future.

She thought of his revelation regarding Uncle Octavius. She understood now why Aunt Harriet had acted so strangely after he had died, as if she were angry. She *was* angry, and for good and sufficient reason. But while Felicity deplored the pain he had caused Harriet and Justin, she could not bring herself to hate her uncle. He had made a terrible and irreversible mistake, but that one mistake was not the whole of his life. He had accomplished much that was admirable and honest too.

She could not hate even Alice, who was the cause of Justin's leaving Felicity now. She felt anger and sorrow that Alice had wounded Justin so terribly. But mostly she felt pity for the woman. Who could guess the private demons that had driven Alice to the desperate life she had led?

And Felicity also could comprehend the emotions that Justin must have had in recovering the Havilland jewels. What dreadful confusion he must have known, attempting to restore honor by the dishonorable act of stealing into houses not his own, rifling through jewel boxes that belonged to others. Engaging in a noble pursuit, all the while forced to behave like a common thief. Or highwayman.

Alice must have given Octavius some trinket of jewelry, which eventually found its way to Harriet. She could not imagine her uncle giving it to her aunt forthrightly. Perhaps Harriet accidentally had come across it, and to cover the true source of the trinket, Octavius had told Harriet he intended it as a gift to her. And at some affair she had worn the trinket, which Justin had undoubtedly seen. It was merely one more of the Havilland collection he must recover.

Suddenly, despite the balmly night air, Felicity went cold. She remembered with sterling clarity the night of her come-out, when Justin had glimpsed her cameo brooch. His gaze had fixed upon it—because it was an unusual piece, he had said. But now, with mounting horror, Felicity realized the true reason. He had recognized her cameo as a Havilland piece.

She yanked back on the reins, her head spinning dizzily. Peter had given her that brooch, and there was only one manner in which he could have come to possess it.

With an agonized cry, Felicity sat upright and clicked her heels into Sheba's side. The mare happily galloped off at breakneck speed, flying over the darkened meadows toward Bellwood House.

She entered through the kitchen, forcing herself to move quietly so as not to disturb any of the household. She would face Harriet and Papa eventually, but first she must speak to her brother.

Silently she crept up to his room, carefully opening the door and slipping inside. Woodenly she walked over to his bed, where Peter lay sleeping.

Dawn was beginning to break, casting gray shadows across her brother's face. She reached out and shook his shoulder. "Peter," she called softly.

He grunted and blinked. Focusing on her face, he roused himself. "Felicity. What . . . ?" Coming more fully awake, he sat up and peered at her.

"Where have you been?" he asked sleepily. "You've set the entire house into an uproar, I can tell you. And what in the world are you wearing?"

"Never mind that now," she told him. "I merely want to ask you one question."

Abruptly her composure broke. "How could you have?" she cried.

"I don't take your meaning."

"I shall tell you my meaning. Alice Havilland!"

Peter gasped and stared at her. "How did you know about Alice?"

"It makes no differeence. Peter! Your friend's wife!"

"I had no idea who she was at the time," Peter said, his eyes imploring her to believe him. "I found out only much later."

"And you gave me that brooch!"

"What else was I to do with it? I met Alice one time, at Vauxhall. She told me her name was Elizabeth something-or-other. I never saw her . . . that way . . . again. Much later, when I discovered her true identity, I was sick. I got drunk for a week."

"And have been slowly drinking yourself to your death ever since," Felicity said harshly.

"You are absolutely correct," Peter admitted, surprising her. "My guilt and remorse have been horrendous. Justin would never forgive me."

His woebegone face melted her heart. "Oh, Peter," Felicity said softly, sadly. "You must forgive yourself, for an unthinking mistake, before your life is in ruins."

Peter smiled slightly. "You know, Lissie, for the first time in my life, I truly want to make something of myself, because of . . . Well. Do you think I can change?"

"Of course you can," Felicity assured him with a tender ruffling of his hair. "Because you are merely turning in your true direction. Oh, dear brother. Write to Justin and apologize. Explain to him that you did not know. Even if he cannot forgive you, you will know you have done the honorable thing in asking for his forgiveness."

For a moment Peter gazed at her, dubious and fearful. Then his shoulders straightened, and a new look of determination smoothed his face. "I shall do it today."

Felicity dropped a kiss upon his brow, then turned to leave.

"One more thing I would like you to do today," she said softly. "Ask Sarah for her hand in marriage. She is so desperately in love with you, she cannot see straight."

Closing the door behind her, Felicity walked slowly to her room. At least on this day, one person in her family would be happy.

21

To her later surprise, Felicity realized that she had fallen into a deep slumber almost immediately, and slept until past noon. When she awoke, Milly was folding the jockey clothing neatly and saying what a clever mistress she had in Felicity. Her father sent a note inquiring solicitously about her health, announcing that he was accompanying Peter and Sarah to the Sumner family residence, hinting broadly about wonderful news and promising to tell her all about their visit later. Felicity went from mystification to total astonishment when, soon after she had arisen and bathed, Aunt Harriet herself brought a tray to Felicity's room. She insisted that her niece crawl back into bed, plumped the pillows for her, and unveiled the covered tray to reveal a pot of tea and no fewer than three of her favorite pear tarts.

Felicity gawked at the tray, and then at her aunt.

"What is it, dear?" Harriet said anxiously. "Would you prefer something else? I shall ring for Cook—"

"No, no, this is lovely. It is simply," Felicity said wryly, "that I expected no more than bread and water."

"What!" Harriet said in mock alarm. "For the cleverest girl in the county? Not upon your life!"

With little prodding, Harriet gladly explained.

At first, when Henning had burst upon them angrily, they all, naturally, had been aghast. But before Sir Edmund departed in a huff, he revealed some interesting tidbits, causing Harriet to check her suspicions against the *Book of Peerage*. Sure enough, it seemed that the gentleman had not been entirely honest with them. A second son of William had settled in the colonies, fought in the American rebellion against the crown, and had become so thoroughly Americanized that he had no interest in the dukedom. But he had never formally renounced the title, and although the man was now deceased, he had a live and healthy son, the rightful heir to William. At any time, the man could show up to claim his inheritance, and Edmund would be out in the cold.

And after the family had realized that Felicity had fled, when they had gone to the stables and heard what she had done, it had been Sarah who had come up with the logical explanation of Felicity's bizarre behavior. Lady Ashford's masquerade ball! Rather an unconventional costume, that of a racing jockey, and naughty of her not to have told them where she was going first, but that was "our Felicity."

"Oh," Harriet sighed, "when I think of how that odious Sir Edmund might have turned us into a laughingstock, I shudder. What a brilliant young lady you are to have seen through the wretch. You know, Felicity, he told us your speech to him nearly verbatim, I suspect. Did you actually threaten to punch him in the eye?"

"I fear that I did," she replied sheepishly.

Harriet laughed with genuine amusement. "Oh, good for you. And I would wager that, had he called you another filthy name, you would have done it."

"I think I actually would have. I was that angry."

Fondly Harriet stroked Felicity's freshly brushed and shining hair. "You know, Lissie, I think that in the end, one is much better off marrying for love, or not at all."

Felicity did not know what astounded her more, the content of her aunt's statement or her use of the childhood name. Harriet had never once called her ''Lissie'' before.

''I married your uncle Ocatavius for love,'' Harriet said softly. ''For many years we were deliriously happy together. But . . . things happen which we live to regret. I angered him, he angered me . . . Still, I am glad I had those happy years. I have come to believe that, all in all, the good outweighed the bad.

''And so,'' Harriet continued, blinking back a tear and smiling, ''I vow that I have given up matchmaking, having barely avoided disaster with Henning. And if you fall in love, you will marry, and if you do not, we will be delighted to have you here. Whatever makes you happy.''

''Oh, Aunt Harriet!'' Felicity cried, throwing her arms about the woman. ''Thank you! I do love you so.''

''Naturally, darling,'' Harriet said briskly. ''After all, we are family.''

And so, instead of the Bellwood disgrace, Felicity had become the heroine of the moment. As relieved as she was, and as touched by Harriet's words, a bleak sense of loss gripped her. She indeed had fallen in love. But she would never marry. Justin was gone.

She rang for Milly to help her dress. But Nanny arrived instead, carrying a parcel that she deposited on the writing table while she laboriously buttoned Felicity into an apple-green afternoon dress.

''Wriggled out of the fire, did ye?'' Nanny asked sourly. ''Got 'em all believin' ye saw through old Henning, when the truth is, ye just brushed him off on a whim to take a midnight ride.''

''Oh, Nanny,'' Felicity sighed. ''It was not as simple as that.''

''Ye know,'' Nanny continued, peering at her, ''ye come

by yer willful ways honestly. Ye're the spit and image of yer mum. And, I was told, she was of the same temper as yer great-grandmama, the one whose second name ye have. The Bellwoods always marry willful women. Or produce 'em. It's all in there.''

Felicity looked at her curiously. ''Nanny, what do you mean?''

Indicating the parcel she had brought, Nanny repeated, ''It's all in there. Yer great-grandmama's journal. Yer mum was like to read it till she wore the pages clean. Gave it to my keepin' the day she passed on, she did, and told me to give it to ye when ye needed it. I expct ye need it now, afore ye get yerself into a tangle ye can't get free of.''

Intrigued, Felicity untied the silk kerchief in which the journal was wrapped. It was bound, not in dark blue and gold, but a soft gray very near to the shade of her own secret journal.

''I'm takin' me nap now,'' Nanny announced belligerently. ''And who's to say I can't? After tearin' me own hair out over Bellwoods all these years, I'm due to live out me days as I please, I am.''

But Felicity scarcely heard her; nor did she notice Nanny taking her indignant leave. She was immediately absorbed in the writing of Mariclaire Bennett Bellwood.

The journal covered the course of the year just before her wedding to Reginald, the sixth earl. Her parents had insisted she marry another, but Mariclaire held out for Reginald. As Felicity read the fervent declarations, the frustration at the obstacles in Mariclaire's path, the passion-filled feelings that were recorded on the pages, she shook her head in wonder. This journal might have been written by Felicity herself.

Hours later, she closed the book with a sigh. So in being her rebellious, freedom-loving self, Felicity had been carrying on a family tradition. For a moment she wondered about those dark blue journals. Had those authors revealed their true selves in the pages, or were they hiding behind what they thought the outer world expected of them?

Hesitantly Felicity went to retrieve her own secret journal from the compartment in the chiffonier in which she had hidden it. For a moment she could not summon the courage to open it. Finally she could not resist.

It was all there, in graceful black-inked script: her laughter and debates with Justin, her railings against injustice, and finally, her doomed love and longing.

Her heart-wrenched tears began to fall, and Felicity was powerless to stop them. But neither did she want Harriet coming upon her in a grief she could not explain to her aunt. So Felicity picked up her parasol and went out to the gardens.

She sat upon a shaded bench, out of sight of the house, enveloped in her memories. They did, indeed, cause her pain, but she would never close them off again. Better to let them into the light, where after a very long time they might not hurt so terribly.

Gradually she became aware of a noise she could not identify. Glancing around, she saw a flash of yellow gown and saw her cousin on the garden path, weeping into her kerchief.

"Georgina!" she called in alarm. "Whatever is the matter?"

Her cousin regarded Felicity in dismay. "Oh, it is nothing," Georgina insisted, approaching with a false smile. "Felicity, are those tears on your cheeks too?"

"It is nothing," Felicity murmured, patting the bench beside her. "Come sit beside me, and we both can weep over nothing."

For a moment they sat in silence, each drying her eyes with a soggy kerchief.

Finally Georgina blurted, "Hubert does not love me!"

"Oh, Georgina, how can you say that? He adores you."

"He may have once, but not now. He pays no attention to me whatever. From morning until night, all that interests him is that silly Exchequer."

"Georgina," Felicity said thoughtfully, "how did you and Hubert come to marry? The true story, that is."

Georgina looked at her guardedly. "What do you mean, the true story?"

"Well, most tales have an official story that one tells to the world in general, and the true story, which may be quite different."

"Oh, Felicity," Georgina said in a low tone, "how did you know?"

"I simply guessed. Tell me."

Georgina smiled bashfully. "Do not ever repeat this, for if Mama ever so much as suspected, she would disown me. The truth is, I proposed to Hubert. I knew that he loved me, and I was mad for him, but he would not make the leap. He is a second son, you know, with no title other than 'Honorable' to his name. Hubert felt he was not good eough for me, and I talked myself blue trying to convince him that he was wrong. Finally I vowed to say that he had compromised me so that he would be forced to marry me. Yes, I actually did! Finally, his knees shaking, so he told me, he went to Mama and Papa and offered for me. They accepted because I had no other suitors on the horizon. In truth, I frightened them all away before they could become serious in their suits. I wanted Hubert, and I got him."

She sighed. "At the start, we were deliriously happy. Then Hubert began spending more and more time at the Exchequer. I tried to gain his attention. Why do you suppose I went visiting all over the country with Mama? I hoped that he would miss me, and demand I return. But he did not. And so I fear that he does not love me after all."

Felicity looked at her in surprise. "Why, Georgina, it's perfectly obvious what the trouble is. Hubert is laboring night and day to make a name for himself and prove that he is worthy of you."

"But that is ridiculous," Georgina protested. "He is worthy of me simply by virtue of who he is, an honest, dear, wonderful man."

"Yes, but Hubert does not have a record of understanding these things on his own. You said yourself that you nearly had to drag him to the altar to prove to him that you loved him. Now you must sit him down and threaten to take out a listing in the *Times* proclaiming your love if he will not believe that he is worthy of you just as he is. Why have you not told him so months ago?"

Georgina shifted uneasily. "It is not the done thing."

"Bother the done thing!" Felicity said bluntly. "Go to him this instant and convince him. You are perfectly capable of that task, Georgina, as you have demonstrated in the past. Make him believe you."

Jumping up from the bench, Georgina said stoutly, "I *am* perfectly capable, am I not?" Slowly, a cunning smile crept over her lips. "But I am not above a bit of special aid in my venture. I think I shall ask Mama to borrow the Cleopatra armlet."

She turned to go, then stopped abruptly and looked back at Felicity in apology. "How rude of me. I did not even ask about your troubles. Perhaps I may help you as you have helped me."

"Thank you, Georgina," Felicity said softly, "but I do not believe anyone can. You see, I—"

"There ye are, milady!" Milly called, bursting upon them. "Searched high and low for ye, I have. This came for ye by afternoon post. Mr. Dobbs says it's marked 'Urgent.' "

Puzzled, Felicity broke the seal and opened the letter.

There were no words on the page. But none were required. With a cry of amazement, and tears, this time of delight, Felicity saw that pressed to the paper were a daisy and a bluebell, their stems entwined.

22

Felicity rode up to the glen just as the sun had descended behind the tree line. Cool, dark green shadows softened the late-summer foliage and shaded the murmuring brook.

Justin must have seen her coming, for he quickly tethered Khan and hurried to her before Sheba had halted. With a joyous shout, Felicity pulled on the reins, and Justin reached up to swing her down from the horse's back. His firm hands closed about the waist of her riding habit and lowered her gently. With the same fluid motion, he pulled her close in a tight embrace.

"You came," he murmured gratefully in her ear. "Oh, thank God. I feared that you might not."

"After the eloquent message you sent me?" She laughed. "A team of horses could not have kept me away."

She drew back, gazing at him, her fingers gently tracing the planes of his handsome face. "You did not leave after all."

"I thought that I could not bear to be so near you without having you. Then I realized that I might roam to the ends of the earth, and still be in agony, knowing that you gazed at the very same moon, breathed the very same air. I simply cannot bear knowing you exist without having you near me."

Felicity rested her cheek on his heart, hearing the steady beat, feeling it pulse in time with her own. "But where did you go last night?"

"I came here," he replied, and somehow she was not surprised. "I stayed until long after the sun rose. And I thought about everything you had said. But even after that, although it broke my heart to leave you, I fully intended to go abroad. All that I could keep of you were a daisy and a bluebell, picked from this glen, where I had first suspected that I might love you."

Justin tilted her face toward him and gently removed her riding hat. One by one, he pulled the pins from her chignon. "I told myself I must go. But all the while, I could still feel the silk of your hair beneath my hands, and smell the rose-water scent of your cheek, and taste the softness of your lips."

Again, one by one, he put his words into deeds. Felicity savored his kiss, a quenching draft of water after such a long thirst. Finally Justin pulled back with a smile and cradled her head in the crook of his shoulder.

"I got as far as the coaching inn," he continued, "and as I was passing, I saw the post coach preparing to depart. And that is when I realized that my love and need for you were stronger than my fear of hurting—and of being hurt by—the woman I loved more than my life."

Justin sighed. "But I did not know if you would even consent to see me, after the unforgivable manner in which I treated you at the masquerade ball. I knew I never could look into your eyes if what I saw there was the loathing I richly deserved. And so I decided to send you the wildflowers by that same post."

"And I," Felicity said softly, "have never received a more priceless gift."

He smiled. "I want to tell you something more. I have

decided to give up tracking down the Havilland jewels. There are still a few missing, but they are not worth the anguish it causes me to retrieve them. It finally dawned upon me that I may stop trying to purge my honor by redeeming the past and begin concentrating on what seems to me to be the most honorable thing I can imagine at the moment: being allowed to love you.''

"Oh, you certainly have my permission," Felicity assured him with a radiant smile. "But I must warn you that I shall never permit you to cease loving me."

"I believe," he answered wryly, "that I shall accept your terms."

A shadow passed over her again, and Justin immediately said, "What is it that troubles you?"

Felicity bit her lip. "I am loath to spoil the most wonderful moment in my life. But there can be no walls, Justin, behind which we hide things that frighten us."

Slowly she reached into the pocket of her riding habit and brought forth the cameo brooch.

"Peter did not know who she was," Felicity said in an earnest rush. "He found out only later, and his remorse has been the reason for his excessive vices. He has been trying to smother the guilt he feels."

"I know," Justin said calmly. "Once my anger with him had run its course, I realized that it could have happened only in that manner. I know Peter so well. Fighting shoulder to shoulder on a battlefield allows one a peek into another's soul."

"And have our battles," Felicity teased him, "allowed you a peek into my soul?"

"Much more than that," he assured her. "I feel that I have walked around in your soul, turning this way and that in fascination, exploring every nook and cranny of you."

"How odd," she said in wonder. "I feel the same sensation about you."

"No more emotional battles between us," he promised her, grinning. "From now on, the only wars that will concern us are the ones that were fought in Troy, ages ago."

"By that great mythical character Agamemnon," she said with a glint in her eye.

"By that great actual personage Alcibiades," he countered in the same spirit.

They both laughed in delighted anticipation. Then Justin took the cameo brooch from her hand and pinned it at the throat of her habit.

"This belongs to you," he declared. "This *is* you, unusual and classically elegant, and undeniably the most beautiful thing I have ever seen."

"Thank you for the brooch," Felicity said tenderly. "It has always been my favorite. . . . Why, I just had the most intriguing thought. This could be the Havilland version of the Celopatra armlet."

Quickly she told him the Bellwood family legend that the armlet brought lovers together.

"Even though the brooch had orgins in tragedy, it did indeed bring us together in the end. I would say that is the most fortunate result that could be. The brooch truly is charmed."

"Well, then," he replied judiciously, "I suspect that there is only one way to seal the legend of the cameo brooch: madam, will you consent to be my wife?"

Felicity sighed happily and threw her arms about his neck. "I thought you would never ask."

He gently tweaked her nose. "Perhaps I was waiting to see if you would ask *me*. Again."

She blushed to remember. "Oh, what a wet goose I was. I had the right idea, that you were the perfect man for me, but the wrong reasons for it. How was I to know that the only reason to wed is for love?''

He looked at her more soberly. ''Will your family agree with you?''

''Oh, yes. For all of what in their minds may be my eccentricities, they all do love me, Justin, and truly wish for my happiness, of that fact I am firmly convinced. They will be delighted that I found a husband who actually may revel in my unorthodox tastes. And be delighted that that husband is you. Peter worships you, you know, partly because of the bond created by your mutual experiences in the wars, and partly, I think, because he senses the valiant and good man you are. And Papa's greatest hero is one who knows fine horseflesh. You rose to inestimable heights in his eyes when you had the foresight to purchase the spring-race-meeting champion right from under his very nose.''

''And Harriet?'' he asked dubiously.

''I think you may be surprised by Aunt Harriet. I believe that over the years she had come to feel that she had erred in marrying Uncle Octavius for love. Because of this love, she had been so deeply aggrieved by him. When she launched her plan to secure my happiness in a loveless but socially and financially proper marriage, she truly did have my best interests at heart. She wanted me to be happier than she eventually turned out to be. But she has seen the error of her mistaken beliefs and now is convinced that wedding a man for love is the only worthy adventure.''

Trailing his fingers through her hair, Justin asked. ''And are you feeling particularly adventurous?''

''Always,'' Felicity owned.

''Well, then, what would you think if I rebooked passage to Venice, but this time for both of us? After we are wedded, we can journey there together. I fancy the idea of wooing you in a more conventional manner in a gondola, under starry skies, with warm Adriatic breezes blowing through your hair.''

"That certainly is conventional," Felicity said with an ironic grin. Then she peered at him eagerly. "Oh, Justin. While we are there, could we pop over to Greece and see the actual sights of the ancient world?''

"I take it that geography is not your strongest area of knowledge. Venice and Athens are not exactly what I would term neighbors.''

"Close enough. Oh, just think of it! We could see the temple ruins and walk on the very ground once trodden by the greatest of ancient Greek military men.''

Justin bent to kiss her, and Felicity realized that no traces of the walls remained, only a clear, open sweep where they each could wander around at will.

"Alcibiades," Justin murmured tenderly.

"Agamemnon," Felicity whispered back.